A Friday Barnes
UNDER SUSPICION

R. A. Spratt

Illustrations by **Phil Gosier**

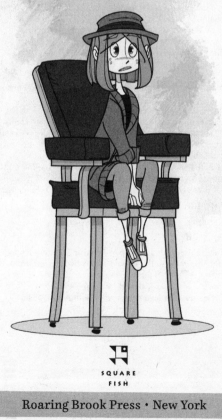

SQUARE
FISH

Roaring Brook Press • New York

SQUARE
FISH

An imprint of Macmillan Publishing Group, LLC
175 Fifth Avenue, New York, NY 10010
mackids.com

Our books may be purchased in bulk for promotional, educational, or business
use. Please contact your local bookseller or the Macmillan Corporate and
Premium Sales Department at (800) 221-7945 ext. 5442 or by e-mail
at MacmillanSpecialMarkets@macmillan.com.

Library of Congress Cataloging-in-Publication Data

Spratt, R. A.
    Friday Barnes, under suspicion / by R. A. Spratt ; illustrations by Phil
Gosier.
        pages ; cm — (Friday Barnes ; [2])
    "First published in Australia in 2014 by Penguin Random House Australia."
    Summary: "The mystery continues in this middle-grade series about a
genius girl detective who solves crimes at her exclusive boarding school"—
Provided by publisher.
    ISBN 978-1-250-14199-6 (paperback)   ISBN 978-1-250-14200-9 (ebook)
    [1. Boarding schools—Fiction.   2. Schools—Fiction.   3. Genius—Fiction.
4. Mystery and detective stories.]   I. Gosier, Phil, 1971– illustrator. II. Title.

PZ7.S76826Frj 2016
[Fic]—dc23

                                                                    2015017839

First published in Australia in 2014 by Penguin Random House Australia
Originally published in the United States by Roaring Brook Press
First Square Fish edition, 2017
Book designed by Kimi Weart
Square Fish logo designed by Filomena Tuosto

1 3 5 7 9 10 8 6 4 2

AR: 5.5

was, what class they were sitting in, and how to do quadratic equations. Whereas Friday was socially clueless, so she relied on Melanie for intuitive knowledge, like telling her when she was being so irritating that her teacher was about to have a brain aneurysm.

Friday had never expected to attend a fancy private boarding school. That was until she received a $50,000 reward for helping her uncle solve a bank robbery. Coming from a highly academic family (both her parents and all four of her siblings had PhDs in physics), Friday decided to invest the money in her education, which was how she came to be at Highcrest.

Since arriving at the elite preparatory school, Friday had gone from being a scruffy eleven-year-old social outcast to being a brilliant eleven-year-old private detective. She'd had to because Friday didn't come from a wealthy family like the other students, so working as a private detective was her way of earning an allowance. Friday was still scruffy and socially outcast, but people were prepared to overlook that when they desperately needed her help.

And Friday didn't just help her fellow students. Even the Headmaster called on Friday when he had a problem he couldn't, or didn't want to, handle himself.

Wrongly Accused

Friday Barnes and her roommate, Melanie Pelly, were sitting in the dining hall at Highcrest Academy, enjoying second helpings of chocolate cake. For two people who had absolutely nothing in common, except their mutual dislike of all sports, Friday and Melanie could not be better friends. They were more than just BFFs; they had formed a symbiotic relationship. Melanie was very vague, so she relied on Friday for basic information like what day of the week it

To Mum and Dad

On this particular occasion, Friday and Melanie were at the end of a long week of searching for a swamp yeti, capturing bird smugglers, and saving the school's reputation, so Mrs. Marigold, the cook, felt they had earned an extra serving of dessert. But their calorie-induced bliss was about to be interrupted.

"Barnes," snapped a voice from behind them.

Friday and Melanie turned around. The Headmaster was standing next to a uniformed police sergeant.

"What's this?" asked Friday. "Am I getting some sort of citizenship award for everything I've done for the school?"

"No," said the Headmaster soberly. "I'm afraid not."

"Friday Barnes," said the police sergeant, "I have to ask you to come with me."

"Why?" asked Friday.

"Because I'm arresting you," said the police sergeant. "You are not obliged to say anything unless you wish to do so, but whatever you say or do may be used in evidence. Do you understand?"

"Not really," said Friday. "Not the situation anyway. But I do have a large vocabulary and as such have no trouble understanding the meaning of your words."

The police sergeant had dealt with people much more intimidating than Friday resisting arrest, so he simply took the matter in hand. He pulled Friday's chair back for her while she was still sitting on it, took her by the elbow, and guided her to her feet.

Friday was mortified. She didn't have to look up to know that everyone in the room was staring at her. This would be yet another reason for all her rich classmates to snigger and laugh at her. There was nothing she could do. She was the most exciting spectacle in the dining room since Mrs. Marigold lost her temper with a vegetarian student-teacher and dumped a pudding on his head.

"If you'll come with me," said the police sergeant,

although Friday could barely hear him through the rushing sound in her ears. People always marvel that holding a seashell to your ear replicates the sound of the sea, but in the seconds before you faint the movement of blood rushing out of your brain replicates the sound of the sea, too.

Friday saw Melanie's concerned expression, and then something made her look across the room. Ian Wainscott, the most handsome boy in school (also the most infuriatingly smug boy in school), was entering through the back door. He was Friday's nemesis/love-interest, no one was entirely sure which. In the past, she'd put his father in prison for a case of insurance fraud

involving a stolen diamond, and Ian had dressed up as a swamp yeti and tried to scare her to death. Yet they seemed to be magnetically drawn to each other, if for no other reason than to bicker.

Friday watched Ian's face as he took in the scene. He seemed surprised for a moment; then he caught Friday's eye, and his face returned to its normal apathetic mask.

The police sergeant started pulling at Friday's arm and the world seemed to return to normal speed. Her ears started to process sound again, just in time to hear the first murmurs of malicious gossip.

It was at times like this when Friday wished she didn't have a brain like a supercomputer. Having a photographic memory meant that the words, and the associated hurt, would be accessible in the long-term storage of her brain's neural matrix forever.

"Typical scholarship kid, probably been stealing," whispered Mirabella Peterson.

"Maybe she's being arrested for wearing those brown cardigans," said Trea Babcock. "She should get five to ten years for crimes against fashion."

"Plus another ten for the green hat," said Judith Wilton.

Now dozens of people sniggered. That was the last

Friday heard as the dining room door flapped closed behind her.

A squad car with lights flashing was parked at the top of the school's driveway.

"The Headmaster is going to hate that," said Friday. "It's a bad look for the school."

"The Headmaster will be grateful I'm taking you off his hands after what y— Wagh!" said the police sergeant, who was interrupted midlecture because he had fallen into a hole about one foot round and one foot deep. "Ow, that hurt," he said, rubbing his knees.

"I wonder who put that there?" said Friday. She inspected the hole. It looked like it had been dug out by hand.

"This crazy school," muttered the police sergeant. "There's always something going on. Rich kids with their weird pranks or bitter teachers with their revenge plots. The sooner we get out of here, the better."

Friday looked back at the main building. She had a lump in her throat and her eyes started to itch. She knew she wasn't suffering from pollen allergies because it wouldn't be spring for another six months.

Friday wasn't terribly in touch with her emotions, but she was able to deduce that she was upset. Being forced from Highcrest Academy was affecting her more than she would have imagined. The police sergeant was entirely right. Highcrest Academy was full of obnoxious children and strange teachers, but it had also become her home. She had friends—well, one friend. And she received three warm meals a day. So despite the Gothic architecture and the even more Gothic attitudes of the staff, this place had made her feel safe and needed—in a way her family home never had. As the squad car started to pull down the driveway, Friday hoped this would not be the last time she saw her school.

The police car wound its way through the rolling countryside to the nearest town. A female police officer was driving. They were heading for Twittingsworth, a fashionable and well-to-do rural area where the weekend homes of city bankers and lawyers were nestled among local farms.

"So what crime am I being accused of committing?" asked Friday.

"We'll discuss all that in the formal interview," said the police sergeant.

"Why, is it some sort of surprise?" asked Friday.

"It's a very serious offense," said the police sergeant.

"We don't want to jeopardize the case by deviating from correct procedure. We're going to do this by the book. There will be a lot of scrutiny. The National Counterterrorism Center has been alerted."

"Counterterrorism!" exclaimed Friday. "But I haven't done anything."

The police sergeant snorted. "Save it for the interview."

The police station was an old stone building, built back in the day when people had taken pride in the appearance of official institutions.

Friday had not been handcuffed. No doubt there were rules about handcuffing children. She also thought it unlikely that her own thin, spindly wrists could be contained by the same handcuffs that would be needed to restrain a fully grown man.

It was the policewoman who led Friday into the building, taking her through to an open-plan area where there were half a dozen desks cluttered with mountains of paperwork. There was one separate office partitioned off at the end of the room, no doubt for the sergeant. There were two doorways on the side. They looked like they led to cells, but they were marked "Interview

Room 1" and "Interview Room 2." A wooden bench sat between them.

Everything inside the police station was gray-green except for the cheerful posters on the wall, featuring famous athletes urging citizens to be respectful of women's rights.

Friday was underwhelmed. She had imagined the inside of a police station to be a more exciting place, but she supposed they could not put up gruesome crime-scene photos on the wall. As a result the police station looked like an average boring office.

Friday sat down on a wooden bench outside the interview rooms. The bench reminded Friday of the one outside the Headmaster's office, although on the whole it was more comfortable. Plus, the police station had less of a feel of impending doom than the Headmaster's office.

On the far end of the bench sat a man who looked like a vagrant, though a strangely large and athletic vagrant. He had been handcuffed to the seat. It was hard to gauge his height because he was sitting down, but he must have been well over six feet tall. He had thinning blond hair and a rough beard. His clothes were old, worn, and crumpled. And Friday noticed that he smelled quite distinctly of mold, even though she was trying her very best not to breathe through her nose. Friday felt like she had been put next to the lion enclosure at the zoo.

The policewoman bent down to speak to Friday in what she clearly hoped was a comforting fashion. "We've left a message for your mom and dad," she said, "so they should be here soon."

"I doubt it," said Friday. "They never check their messages. They only have an answering machine because they find it less irritating than letting their phone ring."

"How do you get in touch with them, then?" asked the policewoman.

"I don't," said Friday. "I suppose I could send an e-mail to one of my mother's PhD students and ask them to speak to her in person. That's what I did the time I broke my ankle on a geology excursion."

"You did?" asked the policewoman.

"Yes," said Friday. "I needed to let Mom know I wouldn't be home because the rescue helicopter couldn't pick me up from the cliff face until daylight. But I haven't done that for ages, because we're not allowed to have e-mail access at Highcrest Academy.

They have a strict anti-technology policy. They're frightened that students will use handheld electronic devices against the staff."

"Really?" said the policewoman.

"Yes," said Friday. "But students find ways around it. I know a girl who only took art so she could sketch incriminating drawings of her history teacher and mail them to her lawyer."

"This is a problem," said the policewoman. "We can't interview you until a family member is present."

"By 'interview' you mean browbeat me into confessing, don't you?" asked Friday.

"Well, um . . ." began the policewoman.

"It's all right," Friday assured her. "As a fledgling detective, I'd enjoy seeing professionals at work. Will you do 'good cop, bad cop,' or are you doing it already and that's why you're being nice to me?"

"Well, er—" said the policewoman, blushing a little at having been caught out by an eleven-year-old.

"This is exciting," interrupted Friday. "Call my Uncle Bernie. He's an insurance investigator. I'll write his number down for you. He'll come right away. I can't wait to get started."

Chapter

2

The Vagrant

Friday knew it would take some time for her uncle to get to the police station. His office was two hours away, and if he was cross-examining a hostile insurance claimant he might not be able to leave work immediately. So Friday reasoned that she had between two and a half and four hours to fill.

She took out a lollipop and stuck it in her mouth,

then looked around the room. She thought of asking for a crossword puzzle, but since she was very good at those it would probably only fill up five or six minutes.

Friday considered asking if she could read the police files, but she suspected there'd be some privacy law preventing the officers from showing them to a child. Also, it'd probably rub the police the wrong way if she read through their files and solved all their cold cases for them.

Friday glanced at the vagrant at the far end of the bench. He didn't look like the chatty type. He looked more the "hit you over the head with a rusty iron bar" type. Friday decided to leave him alone. She pulled a paperback from her pocket and started to read. She'd only been reading for a few minutes when she realized the vagrant was watching her. He hadn't turned and stared, but he was definitely watching her out of the corner of his eye. Friday looked up at him.

"Good book?" asked the vagrant.

Friday hadn't expected the vagrant to engage her in a literary discussion.

"It is, actually," said Friday. "It's E. M. Dowell's *The Curse of the Pirate King*, the story of a privileged boy who defies his family's expectations and runs away to be a pirate, then becomes enormously successful sailing the high seas and winning sword fights with people who are even more dubious than himself. We have to read it for English."

"They let you read that at school?" he asked. "In my day it was all Shakespeare and Dickens."

"The school is particularly proud of this book because it was written by the great-great-grandson of the school's founder, Sebastian Dowell," explained Friday. "E. M. Dowell is one of the few ex-students to become rich and famous without violating insider trading laws."

"Okay," said the vagrant. He didn't have an expressive face, but he seemed bemused.

"It's very exciting. We're all dying to know how it ends," continued Friday. "There's one more book to go in the series. Legend has it that E. M. Dowell came up with the idea for the whole series while he was at our school and that he wrote the last chapter first, then hid it. Like it was pirate treasure."

"Sounds like a weirdo," said the vagrant.

"Yes," agreed Friday. "Although the literary biographies phrase it differently. Their euphemism is 'eccentric recluse.'"

The vagrant snorted a laugh and went back to staring into the middle distance.

Now that she knew he wasn't terrifyingly dangerous, Friday was curious. "What have they busted you for?" she asked.

"What's it to you?" asked the vagrant.

"I'm up on terrorism charges," said Friday.

The vagrant raised an eyebrow.

"I didn't do it," said Friday. "I'm wrongly accused."

The vagrant snorted again.

"Look, I know I look like a child, mainly because I *am* only eleven years old," said Friday, "but I am actually a successful private investigator. I've solved a bank robbery and thwarted a bird-smuggling ring, as well as lots of smaller cases. Why don't you tell me your story? Perhaps I can help."

The vagrant didn't look at Friday, but he didn't look away either. He was clearly thinking about it.

"I'm waiting for my uncle to get here so I can be interviewed," volunteered Friday. "What are *you* waiting for?"

"Their computer to identify my fingerprints," said the vagrant.

"So you're refusing to tell them who you are?" asked Friday.

The vagrant shrugged. "I didn't do anything wrong, so why should I help them?"

"Interesting tactic," said Friday, admiringly. "But aren't you worried that you'll make them angry by being unnecessarily uncooperative?"

"Cops are always angry whatever you do," said the vagrant. "They have an awful job dealing with horrible people all day long. Time-wasting is the least of their worries. In fact, they quite like it because it increases their chances of getting overtime."

"All right, then," said Friday. "Since we're both stuck here for the next couple of hours, give me something to do. Tell me the details of your case."

The vagrant sighed. He was obviously weighing his options. He seemed to be the type of man who pre-ferred to remain silent when possible.

"They say I stole a blue sapphire bracelet," said the vagrant.

"Did you?" asked Friday.

"No," said the vagrant.

"So why do they think you did?" she asked.

The vagrant shrugged. Then he looked down at his clothes. "Look at me, I'm a bum."

Friday nodded. She sucked her lollipop as she thought about it. Truth be told, she wasn't dressed much better herself. But it is a fact of life that some people can wear un-ironed earth tones and look like eccentric academics, and some people look like hobos who have been sleeping under a bush for a week.

"Take me through the details," urged Friday.

"Some rich housewife was taking a shower and she put her bracelet on the windowsill," said the vagrant. "When she got out of the shower, the bracelet was gone."

"And they immediately arrested you?" asked Friday.

"I was seen by three witnesses as I walked through the field behind the lady's house," explained the vagrant. "Appar-ently, there was a group of bird-watchers hidden in a bush as they observed the behavior patterns of satin bowerbirds. One of them took pictures of me with a telephoto lens."

"That doesn't look good," conceded Friday.

"Also there was an escape at the maximum-security prison yesterday," continued the vagrant, "and they say I look like an ex-con."

"Fair enough."

"So the cops picked me up on the road out of town," said

the vagrant. "And when they searched me they found that I was wearing a prison-issue undershirt."

"Why were you wearing a prison-issue undershirt?" asked Friday.

"I was released from prison yesterday," said the vagrant.

"Oh," said Friday, taken aback. She had started to warm to this vagrant, but now that she knew he actually was an ex-con, she was not so confident of her ability, or the appropriateness of clearing his name. "What did you do time for?"

"I don't want to talk about it," said the vagrant.

"That bad, huh?" said Friday.

"I don't want to talk about it," he repeated.

"Okay," said Friday, "I can see how you would fit the profile for just about any crime likely to be committed in a small country town."

"I suppose I do," said the vagrant.

Friday looked at him with pity. "So let me get the facts straight," she said. "You were released from prison yesterday . . . How did you leave?"

"I walked," said the vagrant. "I walked until I got tired at about ten o'clock. Then I found a nice big bush and curled up underneath it to go to sleep."

"Then this morning, you resumed walking?" asked Friday.

"That's right," said the vagrant. "I like walking and being outside."

"And there was a rich lady in town who took a shower," said Friday. "Who knows how long rich ladies take to shower? Probably longer than average, because they wouldn't care about the hot-water bill. So maybe as much as fifteen minutes, or twenty at the outside—she wouldn't want to get pruney fingers. And during those twenty minutes you just happened to be walking through the field behind her house."

"Yes," said the vagrant glumly.

"Where's the bracelet now?" asked Friday.

"I don't know," said the vagrant. "The police can't find it. So they're saying that I took it and stashed it somewhere, planning to come back and get it later."

"That would work," agreed Friday. "Or you could have swallowed it."

"A whole sapphire bracelet?" asked the vagrant.

"You could have put it in a lump of cheese and swallowed that," said Friday. "That's what we did with our cat when we wanted it to swallow a tablet."

"I didn't swallow the bracelet!" said the vagrant.

"Is there any possibility that you did swallow it, but now you have no memory of doing so, perhaps because you subsequently suffered a blow to the head while you were resisting arrest?" asked Friday.

"What makes you think I resisted arrest?" asked the vagrant.

"There's an open first-aid kit on the desk over there," said Friday, "and a red droplet of spatter on the linoleum floor by the doorway, which looks a lot like blood." Friday pointed at the spot without turning her head toward it. She did not care for blood and didn't think that fainting in front of this large vagrant would help her street cred. "Also, there are six desks in this room, but I have only seen two police officers," continued Friday, "which suggests to me that somewhere in this building there is a police officer receiving medical attention."

"I didn't hurt anyone," said the vagrant. "The officer tore his pants when he leaped over a barbed-wire fence trying to chase after me. He got a nasty scrape on his backside. They took him to the doctor for a tetanus injection."

"Hmm," said Friday. "You do make an excellent suspect. You even look dangerous and untrustworthy."

"I know," said the vagrant.

"With so much circumstantial evidence, and your criminal record and frightening physical appearance working against you," continued Friday, "you could quite easily end up back behind bars for this."

"Humph," said the vagrant. "You're making me wish I hadn't started talking to you."

"The only thing that will clear your name is finding the bracelet," said Friday.

"If you do, there's a big reward," said the vagrant. "Ten thousand dollars to anyone who provides information leading to its recovery."

"It's a good thing I know where it is, then," said Friday.

"You do?" asked the vagrant.

"But first, before I take on a client, I like to know what his name is," said Friday.

The vagrant paused for a moment. It obviously went against the grain for him to volunteer anything. "Malcolm," he eventually said. "What about you?"

At that moment the main doors burst open and Uncle Bernie hurried in. "Friday! What mess have you got yourself into now? Terrorism charges! You haven't been looking up bomb recipes on the Internet, have you?"

"Of course not," said Friday. "I promised the federal agents I would never do that again."

The sergeant emerged from his office. "Mr. Barnes, I'm Sergeant Crowley," he said. "If you'd both step into the interview room, we have a lot of questions for your niece."

"What about me?" asked Malcolm.

"It's all right," said Friday. "When they let me off, I'll straighten out your mess, too."

"What if they don't let you off?" asked Malcolm.

"Well, I don't think I'd be a very good advocate for you, then," said Friday as the policewoman led her and her uncle into the interview room.

Deadly Beans

Friday Barnes, you are not obliged to say anything unless you wish to do so, but whatever you say or do may be used in evidence. Do you understand?" asked Sergeant Crowley.

"Yes," said Friday.

"The National Counterterrorism Center received an anonymous letter claiming that you have been making ricin in your dorm room," stated Sergeant Crowley.

"Ricin?!" exclaimed Friday.

"No way!" exclaimed Uncle Bernie.

"Yes, the deadly

poisonous powder derived from the seed of the castor-oil plant," said Sergeant Crowley.

"I know what ricin is," said Friday.

"Of course you do," said Sergeant Crowley. "You've been making it in your dorm room."

"That's ridiculous!" exclaimed Friday. "Why would I do that?"

"We don't claim to understand your agenda," said Sergeant Crowley, "but we know you have a history of this type of thing."

"I do not," protested Friday.

"Do you deny that earlier this year in"—Sergeant Crowley checked his notes—"geography class, your pencil box exploded?"

"Actually, it imploded," said Friday.

"Friday, now is not the time to be pedantic," said Uncle Bernie.

"But it did," said Friday. "And I didn't do it. Why would I implode my own pencil box?"

"Because you were honing your technique," suggested Sergeant Crowley.

"And why would I make ricin?" asked Friday. "I don't have any grudges against anyone. And apart from anything else, it's really hard to make. First, you've got to—"

"Shhh," said Uncle Bernie.

"So you do know how to make it?" accused Sergeant Crowley.

"Of course, I was curious," said Friday. "Isolating lectins is a fascinating field of research."

"This is nonsense," said Uncle Bernie. "Unless you have some evidence, I suggest you release my niece right now before I contact a lawyer about pursuing a complaint for wrongful arrest."

"But we do have evidence," said Sergeant Crowley. "Our crime-scene investigation team locked off her dormitory and went through her room with a fine-tooth comb."

"Urgh," groaned Friday. "You had to do that just before laundry day when the hamper is full of dirty underwear."

Uncle Bernie sighed. "What have you got hidden in your room, Friday?" he asked.

"Nothing," protested Friday.

"We found an unregistered shortwave radio," began Sergeant Crowley.

"I use that to talk to Uncle Bernie," said Friday. "It's important to stay in touch with family."

"Military-grade night-vision binoculars," continued Sergeant Crowley.

"I sleep in a building with two hundred teenagers," said Friday. "It would be stupid not to have night-vision binoculars."

"And a cavity drilled into the handle of your field hockey stick, containing ricin," said Sergeant Crowley.

Uncle Bernie laughed. "Well, then there's no way this can possibly be true. Friday would never own a hockey stick."

"Actually, I do," admitted Friday. "You have to. It's essential school equipment."

An officer came into the room carrying a large plastic bag with a field hockey stick inside.

Uncle Bernie scooted his chair back, away from the table. "Is that thing safe?" he asked. "Even the tiniest particle of ricin is superdangerous."

"Ask your niece, she's the expert," said Sergeant Crowley. "Do you deny this is your stick?"

Friday leaned in for a closer look. "It's definitely mine. It's got a nick in the paint from when I tried to squash a spider but accidentally hit a light fixture instead. Also, it's got my name across the handle in my handwriting."

"And do you deny that these are ricin seeds?" asked Sergeant Crowley, producing a small plastic bag. It had been vacuum-sealed in thick plastic and ziplocked inside another plastic bag.

Uncle Bernie scooted his chair all the way back so that he was wedged up against the far wall. "This is crazy," he cried. "If that's ricin, we're all in danger."

Friday peered at the bag for a moment, then burst into laughter.

"What are you laughing about?" asked Sergeant Crowley. "This is a very serious matter."

"You haven't got very good crime-scene investigators, have you?" said Friday. "Let me guess—you got the two most junior officers on staff to go through my things. You probably weren't expecting to find anything and were shocked when they did."

"So you admit it!" accused Sergeant Crowley.

"I don't admit anything," said Friday. "That's my hockey stick. But I didn't drill a hole in the handle and I didn't put those beans in there. And even if I did, who cares? They're only beans."

"Beans that can be used to make ricin, one of the deadliest substances known to man," said Sergeant Crowley.

"Electricity is deadly," said Friday, "and you've got

two power sockets in this room. But no one is arresting *you*."

"Why did you hide them in your hockey stick?" demanded Sergeant Crowley.

"I didn't," said Friday. "I've been set up. And by someone with a perverse sense of humor."

"I don't see what is funny about a terrorist threat," said Sergeant Crowley.

"It's funny, because not only is this not ricin—it's not even the castor seed that ricin comes from," said Friday, picking up the packet. "These are pinto beans. They look a lot like castor seeds but are entirely harmless. In fact, if you've ever had a burrito, you've probably eaten them, because pinto beans are the main ingredient in refried beans, a feature of Mexican cooking."

"How do I know you're not lying?" asked Sergeant Crowley.

"You don't," said Friday. "You'll have to check with a botanist or a Mexican chef. Or you could wait until the counterterrorism officers get here and ask them to run it through their forensic process. You should—it will give them a good laugh."

Sergeant Crowley drummed his fingers on the desk

for a few moments, then got up and walked over to the door. He opened it and leaned out. "Harris?" he barked.

"Yes, boss," replied Harris.

"Run down to the taco place next to the sports bar and get the chef back here, pronto," ordered Sergeant Crowley. "And when I say run, I mean run, now!"

Six minutes later, Jorge, a short-order chef from Guadalajara, cleared Friday's name by confirming that the bag did indeed contain pinto beans. Sergeant Crowley immediately called the counterterrorism officers and told them to turn back—it had been a false alarm.

"You can go now," said Sergeant Crowley sulkily.

"Do you want to make a complaint about wrongful arrest?" Uncle Bernie asked Friday. "We could pick up the forms while we're here."

"No, of course not," said Friday. "I've had a wonderful afternoon. I want to thank Sergeant Crowley. It's been very educational. And it got me out of woodshop. So it was win-win for me."

"I can have an officer drive you back to school," offered Sergeant Crowley.

"No, thank you," said Friday.

"I'll drive her," said Uncle Bernie.

"No, I mean I don't want to go," said Friday.

"You're not going to confess to something else, are you?" groaned Uncle Bernie.

"No, I want to help Malcolm," said Friday.

"Who's Malcolm?" asked Sergeant Crowley.

"My friend outside," said Friday.

"What friend?" asked Sergeant Crowley.

"The gentleman you've got handcuffed to the bench," said Friday.

"You mean the escaped prisoner and thief we've got handcuffed to the bench?" said Sergeant Crowley.

There was a knock at the door. The policewoman ducked her head into the room. "Boss, I just got a fax from the prison. Our suspect doesn't match their physical description."

"Are you sure?" asked Sergeant Crowley.

"Our suspect is six foot five and has blue eyes," said the policewoman. "The guy who climbed over the wall this morning is five foot four and has brown eyes. Also, the escapee is only twenty, and that's about twenty years younger than the guy we've got."

"Okay," said Sergeant Crowley. "So he's just a bum who stole a bracelet."

"He didn't steal the bracelet, and I can prove it," said Friday, "if you take me to the scene of the crime."

Sergeant Crowley sighed. He would've liked to have gone to the sports bar, or at least the taco bar. All that talk of refried beans had made him hungry. But solving the only other pressing matter on his plate that day would make things easier for him in the long run. Plus, he suspected that if he didn't cooperate, Friday would only embarrass him again.

4

The Real Culprit

Friday, Uncle Bernie, Sergeant Crowley, and Malcolm all stood in the field at the back of Mrs. Knox's house. Mrs. Knox was the well-to-do lawyer's wife whose bracelet had been stolen. Strictly speaking, the field was a park. But the town council had not gone to much trouble to turn it into what people normally think of when they hear the word "park." It was just a field with grass and a few trees, which was actually rather nice. Friday could see why the wealthy Mr. and Mrs. Knox would choose a house overlooking this greenery.

"So why were you walking this way?" Friday asked Malcolm.

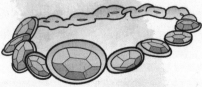

"Because he was looking for houses to break into," said Sergeant Crowley, rolling his eyes.

"I didn't want to walk down the main street," explained Malcolm. "I didn't want to be stared at. I was just cutting through the town along the backstreets."

"Where were you headed?" asked Friday.

"I've got a place a few miles northwest of here," said Malcolm.

"Really?" said Friday. "That would be near our school, Highcrest Academy. Have you heard of it?"

"It rings a bell," said Malcolm.

"Mrs. Knox is expecting us," said Sergeant Crowley. "Are we going to look at the house or not? I've been yelled at by her enough this morning. I'd like to minimize the amount of yelling she does at me this afternoon."

"Of course," said Friday. "Lead the way."

Sergeant Crowley took them through a gate in Mrs. Knox's back fence and across the yard. There was a deck at the rear of the house. Mrs. Knox was standing there, waiting for them. "Is this the vagabond?" she asked on spotting Malcolm.

"The suspect," said Sergeant Crowley.

"The *alleged* suspect," corrected Friday.

"Give me my bracelet back!" demanded Mrs. Knox.

"He doesn't have it on him," said Sergeant Crowley.

"He's probably sold it already," accused Mrs. Knox.

"He doesn't have any cash on him either," said Sergeant Crowley.

"You should be ashamed," accused Mrs. Knox.

"Please don't harass the suspect," said Sergeant Crowley.

"I'm not," said Mrs. Knox, turning on the sergeant. "I'm talking to you. *You* should be ashamed. What sort of police force are you running here, if this type of miscreant is allowed to wander the streets?"

"Can you show me where the bracelet was?" asked Friday.

"Who's this?" asked Mrs. Knox. "Have you invited a schoolgirl to come and have a looky-loo around my home?"

"She's my legal counsel," said Malcolm.

"Ha!" scoffed Mrs. Knox. "Still, I suppose I should be happy you've chosen an adolescent to represent you. It should make the trial nice and quick." She opened the back door and walked in. Everyone else followed. "The bathroom is here."

Friday, Uncle Bernie, Sergeant Crowley, and Malcolm

entered. It was large for a bathroom, but even the largest bathroom is never really a large room, so with everyone standing there it was very cramped.

Friday squeezed her way over to the window. "And this is where you left your bracelet?" she asked.

"Yes," said Mrs. Knox, "I always take my jewelry off and put it there. Normally I wouldn't expect the local police to allow prison escapees to roam around my back garden."

"He didn't escape," said Sergeant Crowley. "He was released."

"Well, that is just a sad reflection on the incompetence of the parole board," said Mrs. Knox.

Friday looked closely at the windowsill. "Did you find any fingerprints?" she asked.

"Only from Mrs. Knox," said Sergeant Crowley. "But that is consistent. He wouldn't need to leave fingerprints to pick up a bracelet. Besides, it was cold this morning and he had gloves in his pocket. Maybe he was wearing those."

"Mrs. Knox," said Friday, "could you describe the bracelet for me, please?"

"It was a sapphire bracelet," said Mrs. Knox. "It had a platinum chain setting and nine brilliant blue sapphires."

"Hmm, I see," said Friday as she looked out across the backyard. "Give me a boost, Uncle Bernie."

"All right," said Uncle Bernie, interlacing his fingers and holding them for Friday to step into, then boosting her up so she could clamber onto the window frame.

"Do you mind?" exclaimed Mrs. Knox, before turning on the sergeant. "How dare you bring a preteen into my home and allow her to stand on my paintwork!"

Sergeant Crowley rubbed his forehead. What with the terrorist false alarm and now this, he was not having a good day.

Friday grabbed hold of the top of the window frame and awkwardly stood up on the windowsill. Because she was taller than the window was high, her head was outside the wall of the house, which meant she was precariously balanced.

"What is she doing now?" demanded Mrs. Knox.

"If you want your bracelet back," said Uncle Bernie, "you'd best just leave her alone. She's good at this type of thing."

"What, irritating people?" asked Mrs. Knox.

"Yes, but also solving mysteries," explained Uncle Bernie.

Friday stood on the windowsill for some time, scanning first left to right, and back again. Then she ducked her head back inside. "Mrs. Knox, have those acacia bushes behind your pool house been there for long?"

"What, those green bushes? Yes, I suppose so," said Mrs. Knox. "The gardener planted them the year before last."

"I know where the bracelet is," said Friday. She leaped out of the window and landed heavily on the damp lawn. "Ow!"

"Friday!" exclaimed Uncle Bernie. "Are you okay?"

"Yes," said Friday. "The ground was just a little bit farther away than I thought."

"Depth perception is not a great strength in her family," Uncle Bernie explained to the others.

Friday scampered down the garden, around the pool, and behind the pool house, disappearing into the acacia hedge.

"One forgets how insufferable children are," said Mrs. Knox. "This is precisely why Mr. Knox and I decided to have none of our own."

Sergeant Crowley, Uncle Bernie, Malcolm, and Mrs. Knox hurried out of the house in the more conventional manner, by using the back door.

When they got down to the acacia bushes, Friday was waiting for them impatiently. "Hurry up," she said. "This is exciting. Like a pirate treasure hunt. Come on." She pushed aside two branches and disappeared into the hedge.

"She can't seriously expect us to follow her," said Mrs. Knox. "What will my hairdresser say if he finds out I have literally been dragging myself through a hedge?"

"I've found it!" called Friday from the far side of the branches.

Mrs. Knox leaped into the bushes like a ninja. "Where?" she demanded.

A moment later they were all crouched on the ground around a circle of dry grass and twigs covered in blue milk-bottle tops, blue clothespins, blue pens, and one blue sapphire bracelet.

"It's a satin bowerbird's nest," explained Friday. "Satin bowerbirds collect blue things to decorate their nests, to attract a mate."

"How sordid," said Mrs. Knox with a shudder.

"Not unlike the reasons Mr. Knox gave the bracelet to you," observed Friday.

Mrs. Knox took out a lace handkerchief and used it

to pick up the necklace. "I will take this straight to the jeweler to have it cleaned."

"Are you going to thank Friday?" asked Uncle Bernie.

"What?" said Mrs. Knox.

"It's all right," said Friday. "The reward money will be thanks enough."

"You don't think you're going to get the reward money just for looking in a bird's nest, do you?" asked Mrs. Knox.

"The reward was offered for giving police information that led to the retrieval of the bracelet," said Sergeant Crowley.

"But it was just a bird that took it," protested Mrs. Knox.

"There were no anti-bird clauses in the reward offer," countered Sergeant Crowley. Mrs. Knox had been rude and mean to him all day. He was enjoying himself now. "I suppose you could get a lawyer to help you wriggle out of your commitment, but that wouldn't look very good in the papers, would it? Wealthy woman too mean to reward an eleven-year-old."

"Very well," said Mrs. Knox. "Harold will just have to run up a few more billable hours, I suppose."

A few minutes later, Friday, Uncle Bernie, Malcolm, and Sergeant Crowley were walking back to the police car. Friday had a $10,000 check in her pocket.

"Do you need a lift anywhere?" Sergeant Crowley asked Malcolm.

"I'd rather part ways now," said Malcolm.

"Here," said Friday, holding out the reward check, "you should take this."

"Friday!" exclaimed Uncle Bernie.

"What?" said Malcolm, looking at the slip in her hand.

"You need it more than me," said Friday. "My school fees are paid up to the end of semester already."

"I can't take your money," said Malcolm.

"Sure you can," said Friday. "I've only had it for two minutes. I'm not emotionally attached to it yet."

"She'd only spend it on something silly, like a centrifuge or something," said Uncle Bernie.

"I said no!" growled Malcolm before stomping off.

Sergeant Crowley shook his head. "Vagrants are always such complex characters."

A short time later, Sergeant Crowley, Uncle Bernie, and Friday were driving back to the police station.

"How did you figure it out?" asked Sergeant Crowley.

"It was obvious that Malcolm didn't take the bracelet," said Friday.

"It was?" asked Sergeant Crowley.

"Yes, because he never said he didn't," said Friday. "If he had taken the bracelet and cleverly hidden it, then he would have been loudly protesting his innocence, demanding a lawyer, and causing trouble. But the fact that he didn't complain, and just accepted the unfairness of the situation, shows that he saw the accusation as so patently false that it was futile to complain."

"Huh?" said Sergeant Crowley. He was getting confused.

"If Malcolm didn't take it, what were the alternatives?" asked Friday. "Who else was in that empty field at seven o'clock in the morning? Nobody but the birds and the bird-watchers. Add to that the two facts that sapphires are blue and there is a large population of satin bowerbirds in this area. The solution was obvious. I just needed to look for an acacia bush, the preferred home of satin bowerbirds."

Chapter

5

The Prodigal Detective Returns

When Friday and Uncle Bernie drove up the long swooping driveway toward Highcrest Academy, it was getting dark. Friday checked her watch. "Everyone will be having dinner."

"Then you'd better hurry along—you haven't eaten all day," said Uncle Bernie.

"What are you talking about?" said Friday. "I grabbed a doughnut at the police station. That is one cliché I rather enjoyed discovering was true."

Friday pushed open the heavy oak doors leading into the dining room. Even though intellectually she knew it was irrational to be anxious about walking into a room full of middle school students, she still was. The 70 percent increase in her pulse rate, the sheen of perspiration on her forehead, as well as the overwhelming urge to turn and run away screaming were all evidence of that. She braced herself for the inevitable stares and the mean jibes of her peers. They liked to make fun of her when she hadn't done anything; now that she'd been arrested, she was sure things would be much worse.

As Friday stepped into the room and the doors swung shut loudly behind her, a lot of people turned to see who it was. They registered it was Friday, then went back to their meals. There was no staring or whispering.

This naturally made Friday suspicious that she was being set up for a cruel joke. She had watched enough high school horror movies to know that teenagers could come up with some very imaginative pranks involving vast quantities of toilet paper or green slime.

Friday carefully walked over to the food line and received her serving of shepherd's pie and peach cobbler, then spotted Melanie on her own in the far corner staring absently into the distance. Friday walked over and slid onto the bench alongside her.

"Oh, you're back," said Melanie. "I'm so pleased. School is a lot harder when you're not here. I was half an hour into third-period physics before I realized I don't study physics and I'm not a sophomore. Then I couldn't remember where I should be and I got in trouble for taking a nap in the rose garden."

"I'm pleased to be back, too," said Friday. "It was fun being taken in and questioned. But I would have been very upset if they'd kept me so long that I missed out on Mrs. Marigold's peach cobbler."

"It's a particularly good one today," said Melanie. "She went heavy on the cob and light on the peach."

"I must say," said Friday, "I'm surprised there isn't more of a fuss over my return. I was arrested and taken away on terrorism charges this morning."

"That was all the buzz for a bit," said Melanie. "But your arrest is only the second-most-interesting thing to occur here today."

"What was the other thing?" asked Friday.

"We've got a new boy," explained Melanie.

"And that's a bigger deal than my being arrested?" said Friday.

"Oh yes," said Melanie. "You know how superficial people are. Plus, you do insist on wearing those ugly brown cardigans and that weird green hat, so being dragged off to face a counterterrorism task force seemed to make complete sense. The only surprise was that it hadn't happened earlier."

"I see," said Friday.

"Whereas," continued Melanie, "the new boy is cute."

"Cute?" asked Friday.

"Totally," qualified Melanie.

"Cuter than . . ." began Friday.

"Your boyfriend, Ian? Yes," stated Melanie.

"Ian isn't my boyfriend," argued Friday.

"No, of course not," agreed Melanie. "Not yet. But it's only a matter of time."

"In fact, I am very angry with Ian," said Friday.

"Oh good," said Melanie. "A feisty argument is a fun way to spice up a relationship."

"Where is he?" asked Friday.

Melanie did not get a chance to answer.

"Friday." Ian was standing behind her.

Friday stood up, which was hard because she was sitting on a bench, so the table was in the way and she couldn't really stand up straight.

Ian smiled, which only made him look even more handsome. This irritated Friday. It's hard to be mad at someone who is distractingly good-looking. She stepped out from behind the bench so she could regain some dignity, and then glowered at Ian. Although it's hard to glower effectively at someone who is ten inches taller than you.

But Ian just smiled again. This time it was his rueful smile, which was arguably in his top three handsomest smiles, even above his "Aren't I charming?" smile and his "You'll forgive me, won't you?" smile.

Friday realized she really must stop categorizing his smiles. It was almost as if Melanie's constant talk of her being in a relationship with Ian was making her subconsciously think it was true.

"Why did you do it?" asked Friday.

"Do what?" asked Ian.

"Don't beat about the bush with me," said Friday.

"I thought you liked intrigue," said Ian.

"Why did you set me up and rat me out to the police?" asked Friday.

"He framed you?" asked Melanie. "How do you know?"

"Who else would go to the trouble of hollowing out the handle of my hockey stick and filling it with beans that look like they make ricin but actually make a delicious burrito filling?" asked Friday.

"I would have thought there were quite a few possibilities," said Melanie.

"Like who?" asked Friday.

"Lots of people dislike you," said Melanie.

"They do?" asked Friday, trying not to feel hurt.

"The Headmaster might have done it," suggested Ian, "to get rid of you because you're a huge thorn in his side."

"Or the Vice Principal might have done it," added Melanie, "because he thinks you're morally dangerous and a blight on the school."

"Or Mrs. Marigold might have done it," added Ian, "because you wrote a formal letter to the school council expressing your concern that the kidneys in her kidney pie were contaminated industrial waste."

"But as far as pranks go," continued Melanie, "this one sounds unusually labor-intensive and imaginative. Just the type of thing Ian would do, what with him being secretly in love with you."

"Exactly," said Friday.

Ian raised an eyebrow.

"I mean 'exactly' to everything except the secretly-in-love part," said Friday.

"But if he wasn't secretly in love with you, he wouldn't bother," said Melanie. "He'd just put itching powder in your gym shorts and be done with it."

"Melanie," said Ian with a smile, "I would never put itching powder in Friday's gym shorts. I know she never attends gym class, so that would be pointless."

"Of course," agreed Melanie. "You really do know each other so well. You're the perfect couple."

"But to report me to the National Counterterrorism Center!" said Friday. "That's just vindictive."

"I thought you said you enjoyed being arrested," said Melanie. "You found it very interesting."

"That's not the point!" said Friday. "Ian didn't know that. And besides, I got lucky. They never took me farther than the local police station. If Jorge from the taco shop hadn't been able to verify my identification of the beans, I would have been thrown in jail and locked up for weeks before it was sorted out."

"Maybe that was the idea," said Ian.

"You wanted to scare the daylights out of me, letting me think I was going to prison for life?" said

Friday. "I thought . . ." She had to stop speaking, partly because she could feel herself on the verge of crying and partly because she didn't know what she thought about her strange relationship with Ian. He had a disconcerting effect on her endocrine system.

"You thought what?" asked Ian.

Friday took a steadying breath. "I thought we were getting along better after everything we've been through. That getting attacked by a yeti and locked in a shed in the swamp had somehow brought us closer together. But to do this, it's just . . . it's just plain hateful."

Ian shrugged, but there did appear to be a small touch of shame to his demeanor. "Perhaps it was nothing personal," he said.

"Is that an apology?" asked Friday. "If so, it's the lamest one I've ever heard."

"It's because he's attracted to you but doesn't want to be," said Melanie.

"I am not!" said Ian.

"Also, he resents the fact that you're smarter than him," said Melanie.

"She is not," protested Ian.

"You see how conflicted you make him?" said

Melanie. "Ian lashes out with cruel practical jokes because his feelings for you make him hate himself."

"What?!" exclaimed Friday and Ian in unison.

Melanie sighed happily. "It's like you're made for each other."

"This is ridiculous," said Friday. "I've been detained, cross-examined, solved a robbery and cleared an innocent man's name today. My brain has already taken in an excess of data. I can't deal with anything else." She turned and marched toward the main doors.

"Can I have your cobbler?" Ian called after her.

Friday looked over her shoulder to glare at him, but as she did, her foot got caught in the strap of a backpack that was lying on the floor. A more coordinated youth would have hopped on the other foot and shaken it off. But Friday was not coordinated. With her head turned one way, her body moving the other, and her foot caught in the backpack, she was unable to remedy the situation. Friday soon found herself traveling at alarming speed, face-first toward the floorboards. She closed her eyes and braced for impact.

But there was none. At least not with the floor. She landed in the firm, strong grasp of a pair of arms.

Friday opened her eyes and found herself looking into merry brown eyes only inches away from her own.

"It's okay, you can breathe now," said the smiling boy.

Friday sighed. She had not realized she was holding her breath.

The boy helped her to her feet. "I'm terribly sorry my bag tripped you up."

"That's all right," said Friday. She was still staring at the boy. He was only a couple of inches taller than Friday, but he looked wiry and strong. He had brown curly hair. A strand of it hung just over his right eye, almost calling to her to reach out and brush it off his forehead.

"My name is Christopher Gianos," said the boy. "I'm new here."

"Friday," said Friday.

"I think it's Tuesday," said the boy, confused.

"No, my name is Friday," explained Friday.

"It's a pleasure to meet you," said Christopher. Then he smiled a disarmingly warm and genuine smile, and shook her hand.

Friday found herself holding his hand for a moment too long. She looked down at it wondering why she wasn't letting it go, but instead found herself observing his strong fingers and the five evenly spaced dots, like a five on a dice, near the base of his thumb.

"Is that a tattoo?" asked Friday.

"No," laughed Christopher. "It's a birthmark."

"Really?" said Friday. "It looks like one of those symbol tattoos that mean something."

"I guess you could argue that a birthmark is a kind of naturally occurring tattoo," said Christopher.

Behind her, Melanie coughed loudly. Friday turned around to see her looking meaningfully at Ian as he walked out the door, letting it slam behind him.

"I've wrapped your dessert up in a napkin," said Melanie. "I know you want to walk away from it now to make a dramatic point about just how angry you are with Ian. But I'm pretty sure you'll regret it at two o'clock in the morning when you wake up hungry and realize you have to wait another six days before Mrs. Marigold makes it again."

"Thank you," said Friday. She turned back to Christopher and found herself staring into his eyes again. "And thank *you*."

"For tripping you up?" asked Christopher.

"No, for catching me," said Friday.

"My pleasure," said Christopher.

Friday walked away with Melanie. There was something about that boy. The way he looked at her. No other boy had ever looked at her that way. Friday glanced back at him. He was still watching her. He smiled and winked. Friday turned away and kept walking with Melanie.

"Does he hate himself for how he feels about you, too?" asked Melanie.

"What?" asked Friday.

"I was wondering if he had a reason for tripping you," said Melanie.

"It was an accident. I stumbled," said Friday.

"It's going to cause trouble," said Melanie, shaking

her head sadly. "Now that Ian has seen you in the arms of another boy, who knows what he'll do next?"

"The police still have my hollowed-out hockey stick, so he can't tamper with that again," said Friday.

"What luck," said Melanie happily. "We've got gym for first period tomorrow and we're supposed to be playing field hockey—now you won't be able to partici-pate! I wonder if I could get Ian to hide something il-licit in my hockey stick, too."

6

More Trouble

As it happened, Friday wouldn't have been able to attend gym even if her hockey stick hadn't been dissected at a criminology lab, because just as she sat down to breakfast she was summoned to the Headmaster's office.

"Can it wait until after breakfast?" Friday asked the messenger.

"He'll yell at me if I go back and ask him that!" said the boy.

"All right," said Friday as she scooped bacon and eggs onto a slice of toast, then stole Melanie's slice of toast to make it into a sandwich. "But

I'm not happy about it. I would have thought that a man with the Headmaster's girth would appreciate that breakfast is the most important meal of the day."

When Friday arrived at the Headmaster's office the door was shut. She had been sent to see the Headmaster many times before, so she took a seat on the now-familiar bench. She wished she had brought her copy of *The Curse of the Pirate King* with her. The Headmaster could, depending on what mood he was in, make a person wait a considerable amount of time. Friday suspected he had some sort of microscopic camera hidden in the corridor so he could see whoever was on the bench while he sat inside his office eating chocolate cookies and watching them sweat.

Friday looked around at the hallway. The tan carpet was institutionally generic. The walls and ceiling were a creamy white, which may have looked nice when they were first painted, but now the crispness of the color only served to highlight the presence of spiderwebs on the ceiling and smudged fingerprints on the walls. Opposite the bench hung the Highcrest Academy honor boards. These were huge plaques crafted out of dark wood with the names of all the top honor students painted in gold leaf. Friday supposed they were put there specifically to intimidate the students on the opposite end of the achievement spectrum, who found themselves regularly sitting on this bench.

Friday ran through the list of names, wondering the gender of the honor students: J. V. Patel, H. C. Baumgartner, E. M. Dowell, A. J. Dean, S. M. Lau, S. J. Santat . . .

Really, reflected Friday, *if they wanted to make the honor board interesting, they should include more detail than the year, initials, and surname. All people have at least one peculiar fact about them that makes them inherently interesting. It would be much more fun if the honor board read . . .*

1990 J. V. Patel, allergic to peanuts

1991 H. C. Baumgartner, direct descendant of Kaiser Wilhelm

1992 E. M. Dowell, will one day be superfamous novelist

1993 A. J. Dean, will one day be incredibly annoying vice principal

1994 S. M. Lau, can fit three hot dogs in his mouth simultaneously

Friday couldn't understand why being top of the class didn't warrant a photograph. If soulless shops went to the trouble of putting up a photo of their star employee of the month, would it kill the school to put up a snapshot of each of the honor students? The honor board couldn't be more anonymous, with its list of surnames and initials. It was limp with lack of meaning.

Just then the door burst open.

"Barnes," barked the Headmaster. "Is that you I can hear breathing in the corridor?"

"Yes, it's me," said Friday.

"Harrumph," grunted the Headmaster. "You'd better come in, I suppose."

Friday sat down in the chair opposite the Headmaster's desk and wondered if she could get away with eating her bacon-and-egg sandwich in front of him. She could feel the eggs soaking through the pocket of her cardigan. The sandwich wouldn't taste as good when it had lint stuck to it.

"What do you know about these holes?" asked the Headmaster.

"What?" asked Friday.

"Holes," said the Headmaster. "Concave indentations in the ground. They've been popping up all over the school. Some student or staff member must have a cockeyed reason for doing it. Although what that might be is beyond me. Anyway, it's a problem. Two students fell in holes this morning, which is bad enough. But I dread a member of the staff breaking

their ankle. The teachers' union has me on proba-
tion already for forcing the staff to chaperone school
field trips."

"But all schools require teachers to chaperone ex-
cursions," said Friday.

"The teachers' union argues that the students at
this school are so conceited and entitled that forcing
teachers to mind them in an unstructured environ-
ment is an act of mental cruelty," said the Headmaster.

"They've probably got a point," conceded Friday.

"I suppose I'll have to talk to Ian Wainscott,"
said the Headmaster.

"What's Ian got to do with it?" asked Friday.

"He's the captain of the golf team," said the Headmaster. "Handicap of two. Excellent swing. But the
team has been complaining for months that they want
a course built on school grounds. Perhaps they've
taken matters into their own hands."

"It's an interesting hypothesis," said Friday. "I can
just see Ian as a vigilante golf-course constructor."

"Anyway, that's not the point. The reason I called
you here is because I've been on the phone all morning," grumbled the Headmaster.

"Oh dear," said Friday. "Was it your bookie? Have you taken up gambling again?"

"No! I was listening to complaints from parents," said the Headmaster.

"About the poor academic standards of the school?" guessed Friday.

"What?" asked the Headmaster.

"Nothing," said Friday.

"The complaints have been about me harboring a terrorist in the student body," said the Headmaster.

"Who?" asked Friday.

"You," said the Headmaster.

"Me?" said Friday. "But I was wrongly accused—framed, in fact. I've been completely cleared. I was the victim of a nasty prank."

"Yes, well, there has been a lot of talk of smoke and fires," said the Headmaster meaningfully. "Also, the parents at this school are not great believers in letting truth or reality cloud their judgment."

"What do you want me to do about it?" asked Friday.

"What I'd really like to do is suspend you," said the Headmaster.

"But I haven't done anything wrong!" exclaimed Friday.

"Are you sure?" asked the Headmaster. "Not even a tiny violation such as sneaking out after lights-out? Copying someone else's homework, perhaps?"

"I'm the smartest student at this school. Why would I copy someone else's homework?" asked Friday.

"Point taken," agreed the Headmaster. "It's just that if I could be seen to be doing something about you, even for a few days until this whole thing blows over and the next imaginary crisis distracts everyone, it would make my life easier. Wouldn't you like to go home for a bit?"

"No, I would not," said Friday. "The food is much better here than at home. For a start, there is actual food here. My parents are physics professors; they get so caught up with quasars and string theory that they forget to go grocery shopping for weeks. They'll get themselves a sandwich from the vending machine at work, but they never think to get one for me. No way, I'm staying."

"We could get Mrs. Marigold to pack you a supply of precooked meals," urged the Headmaster.

"I'm not going anywhere," said Friday decidedly. "I didn't do anything, so I shouldn't be punished. I pay a lot for my education and board. I intend to get value for my money."

"You got a windfall solving a bank robbery," said the Headmaster. "It's not like you scrubbed floors for years to save that money."

"I could have spent it on something frivolous," said Friday. "Like a pony or clothes or, worse, shoes. I chose to invest in my education."

"Yes, yes, you're right, of course," agreed the Headmaster. "But sometimes with these parents it's easier to just compromise all your principles and give in to their unreasonable demands. But it's quite all right if you don't want to."

"Don't you usually just ignore complaining parents?" asked Friday.

"Yes, but I'm under pressure," said the Headmaster. "A member of the school council thinks I'm a tired old has-been and wants to have me replaced by Vice Principal Dean."

"Really?" said Friday. "Which member of the school council?"

"Vice Principal Dean," said the Headmaster.

The telephone on the Headmaster's desk started ringing.

"Excuse me a moment," he said, picking up the phone. "Yes? . . . What? Have you called an ambulance? Good, I'll be right there." The Headmaster hung up.

"What happened?" asked Friday. "Has someone fallen into another hole?"

"No, worse. A huge seed pod from a bunya-bunya pine has fallen on Mr. Pilcher's head," said the Headmaster. "He's unconscious."

"A bunya-bunya pine?" said Friday. "I thought they only grew in Australia?"

"They do, normally," said the Headmaster. "The first Headmaster of the school was quite the botanist. He planted several rare exotic specimens about the grounds."

"Really? This school just keeps getting stranger and stranger," said Friday. "Poor Mr. Pilcher! Bunya-bunya pinecones can be huge."

"I'd better get down there and see for myself," said the Headmaster. "I hope it's not serious. Otherwise our insurance company will want us to cut all the trees down."

"Can I come with you?" asked Friday.

"Yes," said the Headmaster. "And be sure to tell anyone who asks that I am personally keeping you under close surveillance until you have been cleared by the CIA."

"Is the CIA investigating me?" asked Friday.

"I doubt it," said the Headmaster. "But it sounds good, doesn't it?"

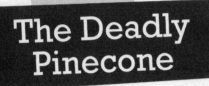

Chapter 7

The Deadly Pinecone

Friday and the Headmaster trudged across several damp playing fields to get to the caretaker's shed. The shed was a large corrugated-iron building that housed several impressive-looking machines: a tractor, a ride-on lawn mower, and a whole wall rack full of hand tools.

A crowd of a dozen or so students plus their young teacher were gathered at the far end of the building. The Headmaster puffed himself up as he approached, ready to assume authority. "Out of the way, boys," he called.

The boys stepped aside to let the Headmaster and Friday into their circle.

There on the ground was the caretaker, completely unconscious. There was no blood, but there was a scattering of large triangular pine seeds all around his head.

Friday looked up at the huge tree that towered over them. It had massive pinecones the size of watermelons, and when they hit the ground they shattered like hand grenades into triangle-shaped seed pods the size of a fist.

"That must have hurt," observed the Headmaster.

"Yes, indeed," agreed Friday. "A bunya-bunya pinecone can weigh up to ten kilograms. To have that hit you on the head accelerating at thirty-two feet per second over a hundred-and-thirty-foot drop—allowing for the fact that Mr. Pilcher is about five feet nine inches tall and collapsing to the ground would absorb some of the impact—it would result in over two thousand one hundred and seventy-seven newtons of impact force slamming into your skull."

"Thank you," said the Headmaster. "I know what I'll be thinking about as I attempt to sleep tonight."

"He's breathing and he's got a strong pulse," said the young teacher.

"That's a miracle," said Friday.

"What happened?" asked the Headmaster.

"I was taking the boys out for their cross-country training," explained the teacher. "It was Gillespie who found him. He's our fastest boy. We've got high hopes for him at the regional track meet."

Gillespie blushed at the praise.

"Yes, yes," said the Headmaster. "But did anyone see what happened?"

"No, sir," said Gillespie. "Mr. Pilcher was lying on the ground, knocked out cold, when I got here."

"When was that?" asked Friday.

"Ten minutes ago," said the teacher.

Friday crouched down and inspected the caretaker herself. She looked at his fingernails. The tread of his boots. The hems of his trousers. And she even smelled his breath.

The older boys were disgusted. "Ew, gross."

The Headmaster rolled his eyes. "Barnes, must you always sniff things? You know it's behavior like this that makes you such a credible suspect for the police."

"It's behavior like this that got me and a swarthy ex-jailbird off when suspected by the police," said Friday as she grabbed Mr. Pilcher by the arm, pulled his knee up, and rolled him over onto his side.

"What are you doing?" demanded the Headmaster. "You shouldn't touch him."

"I thought all teachers had to do first-aid courses," said Friday. "An unconscious person should always be rolled onto their side, into the safety position, so if they throw up they don't choke on their own vomit."

"Ew," chorused the boys again.

"She's right, sir," said the teacher. "I did my first-aid course six weeks ago, and they were very adamant about that."

"Yes, yes," said the Headmaster. "I may have many faults as a headmaster, but I assure you that allowing staff to choke on their own vomit is not one of them."

"Plus," said Friday, "rolling him onto his side allows me to look at the back of his head." She peered closely at the back of Mr. Pilcher's crown. "Just as I suspected," she muttered.

"What did you suspect? That he'd have that enormous lump?" asked the Headmaster. "I can see it from here. That's going to hurt tomorrow."

"Yes, there is an enormous lump," agreed Friday. "That is the lymph rushing to the area with platelets and white blood cells to help heal the wound. But if you look closer you'll see that the back of Mr. Pilcher's head has a lot to tell us."

"Here we go," said the Headmaster, rolling his eyes.

"Does anyone have a sheet of paper?" asked Friday.

The boys were in their running shorts and tanks, so they were of no help. The teacher shrugged.

"Not even a betting slip?" asked Friday, looking meaningfully at the Headmaster.

The Headmaster sighed and took a small slip of paper from his pocket, and handed it to Friday.

Friday laid the paper on the grass under Mr. Pilcher's head. Then she brushed his hair with her hand. A shower of dirt, dried grass, and leaves fell onto the slip.

"That is a lot of organic debris," said Friday.

"He's a groundskeeper," said the Headmaster. "He's got a dirty job."

"But he always wears a flat cap to protect his hair," said Friday. "Besides, if he had simply been hit on the head and fallen to the ground, like so . . ." Friday lay down on the grass for a moment then sat back up. "Can you see anything in my hair?"

The Headmaster looked at Friday's head. There was nothing there.

"You've lost your hat," said the teacher, picking up Friday's green porkpie hat.

"Well observed," said Friday, putting the hat back on her head.

"A man could only get that much debris in his hair if he had been dragged," said Friday.

"Dragged where?" asked the Headmaster.

Friday looked around. "The answer lies with Mr. Pilcher's newsboy cap. Can anybody see it?"

Now all the boys looked around.

"Over there," called a boy. "In the doorway to the shed."

The group hurried over to inspect the hat.

"Stay back!" Friday warned.

The rest of the group stood several feet away while Friday crept forward. She took a pen out of her pocket and carefully picked the cap up and checked the underside.

"Just as I suspected," said Friday.

"What is it?" asked the Headmaster.

"Nothing," said Friday. She looked down at the ground, peering intently, until she dropped to her knees, whipped out a magnifying glass, and closely inspected a blade of grass. Then, just as quickly, she slapped her hand across her mouth and squeezed her eyes shut, as if she were obviously sickened by what she saw.

"Are you going to tell us what you've found?" asked the Headmaster.

"See for yourself," said Friday, weakly.

The Headmaster bent down and plucked the blade of grass Friday had been inspecting. There was a small dark blob on one side of the blade.

"What is it?" asked the teacher.

"Blood," said the Headmaster.

"Precisely," said Friday with a shudder.

"Urgh," moaned a voice.

"It's Mr. Pilcher," said Gillespie.

The group rushed back to the stricken man. As they got there he was trying to sit up.

"It's all right, Pilcher, take it easy. An ambulance has been called for you," assured the Headmaster. As if to confirm this, the faint wail of an ambulance could be heard approaching over the rolling hills.

"What happened?" asked Mr. Pilcher.

"We were hoping you could tell us," said the Headmaster.

Mr. Pilcher rubbed his forehead. "I don't remember

anything. I don't even remember getting out of bed this morning."

"I can tell you what happened," said Friday.

Everyone turned and looked at her.

"Go on," said the Headmaster.

"Mr. Pilcher was not hit on the head by a bunya-bunya pinecone," said Friday.

"But then why is he lying here, under a pine tree, with seeds littered about him?" asked the teacher.

"Because he was hit on the head over there by the shed," said Friday. "When he fell to the ground, his hat fell off."

"What are you saying?" asked the Headmaster. "That one of the tools fell off the wall and hit his head?"

"In a manner of speaking," said Friday. "But only because someone took the tool and swung it at him, then dragged Mr. Pilcher over here, smashed a pine-cone on the ground, and carefully laid his head in the middle of the seeds."

"I don't believe it," said Mr. Pilcher.

"You were assaulted by someone very devious," said Friday. "But they didn't move the hat. The idea of using the pinecone was a stroke of genius. But to leave the hat was an amateur mistake, which leads me to suspect that the perpetrator was interrupted before he could finish staging this miniature perfect crime."

"There's nothing miniature about the lump on Pilcher's head," said the Headmaster. "Why would anyone do it?"

"I don't know," said Friday.

The ambulance pulled up and the paramedics bustled out quickly, taking over.

Mr. Pilcher started fussing about who would turn the compost bin if he was taken off to the hospital. The Headmaster reassured him that no one on the staff or in the student body would perform any of his jobs while he was away, so that everything would be just as Mr. Pilcher had left it, only slightly overgrown, by the time he returned.

Friday stepped back, her attention drifting over to the shed. She went to have a look.

Inside the shed, one entire wall had been made into a pegboard that held Mr. Pilcher's extensive collection of tools and garden implements. An outline of each tool was painted onto the pegboard. And everything was hung in its place, except for one tool: the stencil of a spade was empty.

Friday had found the assault weapon. Or, rather, she had found the lack of the assault weapon. Now she just needed to work out the reason for such a strange attack.

Friday turned to Mr. Pilcher's desk. It was littered with invoices and order sheets. A worn paperback laid open on top of the pile. Friday flipped the book over to see what it was.

"*The Curse of the Pirate King*," muttered Friday. "Hmm, interesting."

Somewhere in that shed lay the motive for the assault, but even Friday's enormous brain could not determine exactly where.

Mrs. Cannon

When Friday finally ran out of excuses to avoid going to class that morning, she was happy enough to go because it was third period, which meant English.

Mrs. Cannon always encouraged them to spend the first twenty minutes of every lesson silently reading. She said this was to improve the students' literacy, but really it was so she could have some peace and quiet to study the job

ads. Mrs. Cannon couldn't do this in the staff room in case the head of the department caught her. But the children were much more understanding about her desire to get out of her career in education. In fact, sometimes she would interrupt their silent reading to ask the children's opinion.

"Here's one," Mrs. Cannon said. "Chef wanted. Grilling skills essential. Must be available to work nights and weekends."

"But you have tango lessons on Thursday evenings," said Melanie.

"You're quite right," agreed Mrs. Cannon.

"And you can't cook," added Peterson.

"No," admitted Mrs. Cannon. "But how hard can it be? It must be easier than being an English teacher."

The children nodded. They would not like to have to teach themselves English either. Then they all went back to their quiet reading until another job would catch Mrs. Cannon's eye.

"How about this one, children?" Mrs. Cannon would interrupt. "Nanny needed to work in Kuwait. Six days a week, room and board provided."

"But, Mrs. Cannon," called a boy, "you don't like children."

"True, very true," agreed Mrs. Cannon.

"And you don't like sweating," added another girl. "Kuwait is a very hot country. A job like that would be sure to involve sweating."

"Good point," agreed Mrs. Cannon.

This is how the lesson would continue until the last ten minutes, when someone would point out that they didn't have long to go. Then Mrs. Cannon would reluctantly put down her paper and launch into a literary discussion, which would always end up with her concluding that the author they were discussing, be it Jane Austen, Charles Dickens, or Arundhati Roy, was extremely lazy for not including more gunfights, explosions, and murder mysteries in their stories. And it was entirely the author's fault if students could not get through the first fifty pages of their books without falling asleep.

On this particular morning, Friday arrived when the job ads were unusually lackluster, so Mrs. Cannon was getting the class to help her with the crossword puzzle instead.

"What's an eight-letter word for the fourth stomach of a cow?" asked Mrs. Cannon.

"Abomasum," said Friday as she walked in through the door.

"Well done," said Mrs. Cannon, filling in the squares. "You're not late because you've done something dreadful I have to punish you for, are you?"

"No, Mrs. Cannon," said Friday. "I was helping the Headmaster."

"Very well," said Mrs. Cannon. "As long as I don't have to fill in any slips or report you to anyone. It was so much easier back in the day when you could just spank a child and get on with your lesson plan. These days everything involves filling in paperwork."

"Did you really cane students back in the olden days?" asked a boy.

"No," admitted Mrs. Cannon. "It seemed like such a lot of effort. First, I'd have to stand up, and you know I dislike doing that. Then, I'd have to catch them. And the wicked things children do always seem like exactly what I would do if I were in the same position, so my heart was never in it."

Friday made her way to the back of the class. Melanie was sitting in her usual seat next to the window, staring out. Friday sat down beside her. The desks were arranged in a horseshoe pattern, so Friday had her back to the window. Looking across the room, she could see Ian smiling his usual smug smile, but then it transformed into a glare. It was an unexpectedly hateful glare. Friday was baffled until she heard a tapping sound behind her.

She turned around to see Christopher standing outside the window, waving to her. Friday glanced across at Mrs. Cannon, who was concentrating hard on her crossword, so Friday slid her chair back toward the window.

Christopher raised the sash. "Hello," he whispered.

"Hello," whispered Friday. She wasn't used to making small talk with boys, so she paused here.

"Friday," said Mrs. Cannon, "if you are going to talk to your friend, please hold a book in front of your face while you do it, in case the Vice Principal walks in."

Friday dutifully took her copy of Proust out of her bag and opened it to the page she was on.

"Proust? Very impressive," said Christopher.

"Oh, I'm not reading Proust," said Friday. "I just cut the cover off my copy of *Swann's Way* and stuck it over a book on forensic psychology. I wouldn't want Mrs. Cannon to get in trouble if I'm caught reading nonfiction in her class."

"I heard that you were the smartest girl in school," said Christopher. "I was wondering if you could help me. I've got to try to catch up with the academic standard here, particularly in geography. Would you be able to meet me sometime to give me a few pointers?"

"Keeping up with Mr. Maclean's class isn't very hard," said Friday. "He barely knows anything about geography himself."

"He's asking you out on a date," said Melanie, turning away from the window.

Friday looked at Melanie, then at Christopher, and then back at Melanie. "Don't be ridiculous," she said. "What makes you say that?"

"What boy would want to catch up with academic work?" asked Melanie.

Friday looked at Christopher. He smiled at her. Friday felt alarmed by this unforeseen situation.

"I'll get back to you," said Friday.

"Okay," said Christopher with a smile.

Friday slid the window shut. "Do you think there's something wrong with him?" she whispered.

"There definitely is," said Ian from the far side of the room. "He's so smarmy. All that fake smiling—it's enough to make you sick."

"I would have thought that, for you, it would be like looking in the mirror," said Friday.

"Good one," chuckled Melanie. "They do both like to smolder, don't they? Although Christopher has more of a twinkly smolder, whereas Ian's smolder is more broody."

"I'm not broody," argued Ian.

"I meant in a nice way—broody like Byron," said Melanie, "not broody like a chicken."

"He's coming!" hissed Peregrine, the boy whose turn it was to sit by the door and watch out for the Vice Principal.

Mrs. Cannon got to her feet and started speaking loudly. "And so through his use of assonance, alliteration, and bottom humor, Chaucer teaches us of the dangers of . . . Oh, good morning, Vice Principal Dean."

The Vice Principal was standing in the doorway, watching the children suspiciously as they dutifully wrote notes in their books. "Is everyone behaving themselves here?" he asked.

"Oh yes," said Mrs. Cannon. "Such a wonderful class. Great lovers of literature."

The Vice Principal scanned the room. Everything was as it should be. Which was, of course, suspicious.

"I've got my eye on you, Barnes," said the Vice Principal.

"Me, sir?" said Friday.

"Yes, you," said the Vice Principal. "Just because the police didn't have enough evidence does not make you innocent in my eyes."

"You don't believe in the fundamental tenet of our judicial system—the presumption of innocence?" asked Friday.

"Of course not!" said the Vice Principal. "This is an elite private school. Brutal arbitrary punishment is our tradition. That's the way it was in my day. And no one was getting arrested for terrorism back then."

"Sir, since you're here and it is our English class you're interrupting," said Friday, "could I ask you a literary question?"

"Me?" asked the Vice Principal. "But I'm a math teacher."

"Naturally," said Friday. "Vice principals usually are. But I thought you could share your unique insight into the author of *The Curse of the Pirate King*, since you were here at school the same time as E. M. Dowell. Weren't you in the year below him?"

The Vice Principal went bright red. It was hard to

tell whether it was from embarrassment or anger, but it was probably a combination of both. "I never had anything to do with that degenerate," he said. "Arrogant little upstart. I don't know why everyone makes such a fuss over him."

"Really? I thought he was a lovely boy," said Mrs. Cannon. "Such a nice smile. Whereas all I remember of you, Vice Principal, was that you were terrible at spelling."

The Case of the Lying Roommate

It was a slow and boring week. Friday and Melanie actually found themselves attending classes and doing homework. Friday was sitting in her dorm room, learning the effects of platypus venom for biology, when the door opened and Trea Babcock walked in.

"I need your help," said Trea.

Friday turned and glared at her roommate. "I thought you said you locked the door."

"Did I?" said Melanie. "I probably thought I did at the time. That's the problem with having Attention Surfeit Disorder—it's hard to distinguish between what you know, what you think you know, and simply what you think, I think." Melanie went back to gazing at the ceiling. This was her second-favorite pastime after sleeping.

Friday tipped back her green porkpie hat and looked at her new client. Trea Babcock was a slim brunette sophomore. She was not terribly nice. She never would have spoken to Friday under normal circumstances. Friday was curious. "How can I help you?" she asked.

"I loaned Jacinta, my roommate, my calculator and she won't give it back," said Trea, clearly distressed.

"It's just a calculator. Why don't you buy another one?" asked Friday.

"I don't want to say," said Trea. "I don't want to incriminate myself."

"I'm not the police or the Headmaster," said Friday. "You can tell me."

"The calculator's a model that is unacceptable under the school's anti-technology rules," said Trea. "It's Wi-Fi capable. I can use it to shop online."

"Your calculator can do online shopping?" asked Friday.

"It's quite handy," said Trea. "You can tally up the purchases while you shop."

"So why not buy another one?" asked Friday.

"Duh," said Trea, "because I'd have to get it smuggled in via the swamp. That's how I got the last one in."

"And how is that problematic?" asked Friday.

"Pedro, our family gardener, refuses to paddle Daddy's dinghy into the swamp again," said Trea. "He fell overboard last time. Then he made such a fuss because he couldn't swim."

"He could have drowned," said Friday.

"I suppose," said Trea. "But Mirabella Peterson's maid was smuggling in her hair-curling tongs on that same night. She pulled him out and knew all about CPR, so he was fine."

"So why won't Jacinta give your calculator back?" asked Friday.

"She says she doesn't have it," said Trea. "I lent it to her last Thursday because she was doing her calculus homework and her calculator's battery had gone flat. But today when I asked for it back, she was so busy doing her art project she didn't even look up. She just said, 'Sorry, I don't have it.'"

"Then what did you say?" asked Friday.

"Nothing," said Trea. "Jacinta put her earbuds back

in and kept doing her sculpture. So I did what any roommate would do."

"And what's that?" asked Friday. She was self-aware enough to know she did not think like a normal roommate.

"I rifled through her things when she left for ballet class," said Trea. "But I couldn't find my calculator anywhere."

"Hmm," said Friday, "I see." She turned to where Melanie was lying in a deeply relaxed meditative state on the bed. "Melanie, snap out of it. We need to go and investigate the scene of the crime."

"Okay," said Melanie. This was her response to most things, even when they clearly weren't okay.

Friday gathered her notebook and Melanie gathered her thoughts as they got ready to leave.

"So you agree it is a crime scene?" said Trea excitedly. She was looking forward to an opportunity to denounce her roommate. She had three months' worth of irritation built up about everything, from the way Jacinta left her dirty socks on the floor to the way she snored like a chainsaw when she had a cold.

"We'll see," said Friday.

"I know she's still got it because Bronwyn Hanley

saw Jacinta with it at lunchtime yesterday. She was in the library doing homework."

"That can't be right," said Melanie.

"What do you mean?" asked Friday.

"Jacinta was at field hockey practice at lunchtime yesterday," said Melanie. "I was sitting in the dining room, staring out the window. I could see her running."

"Melly Pelly, you have a mind like a sieve," said Trea dismissively. "You must have confused her with someone else."

"No, I distinctly remember," said Melanie. "Because Jacinta fell in a hole on the field and went over on her ankle, giving it a bad twist."

"There was a hole in the field?" asked Friday.

"Yes, quite a large one," said Melanie. "Her foot completely disappeared up to the shin. It reminded me of that game you play when you're little, where you don't want to stand on the cracks in the pavement or a lion will get you."

"I always thought it was a crocodile," said Friday.

"Definitely something large that will eat your leg," agreed Melanie. "Which is why Jacinta's leg suddenly disappearing before my eyes made me think of it. They had to carry her off crying. It was very sad. But a good cautionary example of why you should never play sports."

Several minutes later, when they arrived at Trea's room, Jacinta wasn't there.

"That's good," said Trea. "You'll be able to search her things."

"I have no intention of doing that," said Friday. "It would be an invasion of Jacinta's privacy."

"But I'm her roommate," said Trea. "She has no privacy from me."

"Hmm," said Friday, who did not particularly like her client. "Go and stand by the door next to Melanie and be silent. If you find yourself unable to not speak, watch Melanie—she will show you how to do it."

Melanie smiled at Trea silently, which was very kind of her because she didn't like Trea either.

Friday looked around the room. There was no actual line marked on the floor or walls, but there may as well have been because there was a clear difference between the two halves. Trea's half was very neat and all her possessions were pretty: feathery pens, love-heart-covered diaries, and a pink quilt set.

The other half of the room was disheveled, with a

large amount of stuff shoved into the small space: schoolbooks, papers, sports equipment, clothes, and a half-eaten chocolate bar lying on the middle of the desk. There was also an eclectic collection of fiction: lots of classic romance novels by Jane Austen and the Brontë sisters, as well as lots of action-adventure stories by Lee Child and Jo Nesbø. Jacinta's music collection included retro country classics by Dolly Parton and moody alternative rock by The Cure. On the wall were two large posters, one of the great ballerina Darcy Bussell and one of the great female field hockey player Luciana Aymar. There was also a framed picture of a middle-aged couple. Both looked large, proud, and stout.

"They're Jacinta's parents," said Trea. "They're huge in the building industry. They met on a building site. Her dad was a bricklayer and her mom was a quantity surveyor. Can you believe it? They let anyone into this school these days. No offense." Trea patted Friday on the arm.

Friday went over to Jacinta's desk, took out a magnifying glass, and closely observed each item without touching it. "What's this?" she asked, pointing to a long pink elastic bandage snaking its way out of a desk drawer.

"I don't know," said Trea. "A bandage, I suppose. She did sprain her ankle playing hockey, although I'm sure Melanie has her times wrong."

At that moment a girl in a pink leotard and tutu walked in. To be strictly accurate, it was more as if she floated. Her movements were so graceful.

"This is Jacinta," glowered Trea.

"Hello," said Jacinta, not picking up on the tension in the room, because she immediately started looking through her voluminous ballet bag. "Trea, I just realized I've still got this." Jacinta pulled out a big black calculator.

"I knew you had it all along!" exclaimed Trea.

"No, she didn't," said Friday, looking shrewdly at Jacinta.

"What do you mean?" asked Trea.

"Jacinta—if Jacinta is her real name—knows what I mean," said Friday mysteriously.

Jacinta looked nervous. "No, I don't."

Trea was not interested anymore. "Well, that doesn't matter now, because I've got my calculator back." She smiled at Friday. "So I don't have to pay you, do I?" The smile teetered over into smugness. Trea left, bouncing out the door.

"You should have a service fee, like plumbers," said Melanie, "to stop people from needlessly interrupting our homework."

"You were gazing at the ceiling," said Friday.

"Which is an even greater crime to interrupt," said Melanie.

Friday turned back to Jacinta and stared at her as if she were as fascinating as a bloodstained murder weapon.

"Why are you here?" asked Jacinta.

"I solve mysteries," said Friday. "I enjoy it."

"I've returned the calculator, if that was the problem," said Jacinta defensively.

"The calculator barely counted as a problem," said Friday. "There is something much more interesting going on here."

"I don't know what you're talking about," said Jacinta.

"There's no point lying to me," said Friday. "I always proceed on the assumption that everyone is lying all the time, which allows me to discount everything they say."

"I'm not lying about anything," protested Jacinta.

"Yes, yes," said Friday as she walked along with her

ear pressed to the wall, rapping the drywall with her knuckle. "As I said, I'm not listening to you." She went over to the door and looked around in the corridor. "Is that a janitor's closet next to your room?"

"Yes," said Jacinta cautiously.

Friday went down the corridor and tried the door to the closet. It didn't budge. Not even the handle turned. "Someone has put glue in this lock," said Friday.

"Perhaps it was the janitor so he could get out of cleaning the floors?" guessed Melanie.

Friday came back into Trea and Jacinta's room, looked around once more, and went over to the built-in wardrobe. "You don't mind if I open this, do you?" she asked.

"Well, actually . . ." began Jacinta.

But it was too late. Friday had slid open the door and pushed aside the hanging clothes. Then she did the most unexpected thing: she stepped into the built-in wardrobe and disappeared.

"Wow," said Melanie, "you haven't got an entrance into Narnia in your wardrobe, have you? I was really disappointed when I was told that those books were fiction, so if it is in fact real, that would be wonderful."

Just then Friday stepped back out, but this time she was joined by another girl who looked exactly like Jacinta. The same height, the same hair color, the same eye color, and the same petulant frown.

"What's going on?" asked Melanie. "Is your wardrobe a cloning machine? That's even more amazing than a doorway to Narnia."

"This is not a clone," said Friday. "This is Jacinta's identical twin sister."

"Twins!" exclaimed Melanie. "Okay, I can see that is slightly more plausible than Narnia or a cloning machine. But it still does seem very strange."

"Which one of you is the real Jacinta?" asked Friday.

"I am," said the girl from the wardrobe.

"I'm Abigail," said the girl who they had previously thought was Jacinta.

"So you're both here," said Friday. "But you take turns going to classes and sleeping out here in the bed."

"Yes," agreed the twins.

"Why?" asked Friday.

"Yes," said Melanie. "Usually I'm not a curious person, but even I was wondering that."

"For the money," explained Jacinta.

"We figured out how to hack into our father's bank account and divert the payment for one of our school fees to our own bank account in the Cayman Islands," explained Abigail. "That way only one of us would be enrolled. But Daddy would be paying for two."

"And also so we could ditch the boring classes," added Jacinta.

"Yes," agreed Abigail. "I prefer science, whereas Jacinta likes English and history. This way we just go to the classes we like."

"Who goes to math class?" asked Friday.

"Yuck!" said both girls. "Neither of us likes that. So we take turns."

"Wow, you only attend half the classes each," said Melanie. "I think these girls might be even more brilliant than you, Friday."

"What are you going to do with us?" asked Jacinta.

"Are you going to report us to the Headmaster?" asked Abigail.

"Of course not," continued Friday. "You've worked out a brilliant scheme. When I was trying to avoid

going to junior high, I wish I'd thought up something as clever as this."

The girls started to smile. "How did you figure us out?" asked Jacinta. "Surely it was more than just the calculator."

"It was," agreed Friday. "It was several things. First, your taste in literature. You've got Jane Austen and Lee Child. Then, your taste in music. There's Dolly Parton and The Cure. And your interests: hockey and ballet. Everything is diametrically opposed, as if two people were living here. Then there's the fact that you were sighted in two places at once. But the clincher was the pink bandage."

"The bandage?" asked Melanie.

"Yes," said Friday. "How could you injure your ankle playing field hockey yesterday and then go to a ballet class today? You're wearing pointe shoes. That is very hard on the ankles. So obviously it was not those ankles that took the blow in hockey. So there had to be another set of ankles attached to a person who looked exactly like you, which means either a vast amount of incredibly expensive plastic surgery or an identical twin. Given the increasing birthrate of twins, I judged that was the more likely scenario."

"Brilliant," said Melanie.

"Then it was a question of where," said Friday. "The janitor's closet next door was the obvious choice. I soon discovered the door wasn't just locked, it was glued shut. Someone had injected glue into the lock mechanism. With that doorway blocked, it would be easy for two girls who were heiresses to a building empire to access the power tools and materials necessary to cut another secret doorway through their wardrobe into the janitor's closet."

"So what happens now?" asked Abigail. "Are you going to tell our parents?"

"Goodness, no," said Friday. "I'm not the police. Good luck to you. If I had to share a room with Trea, I'd be glad for a secret room in the back of my wardrobe, too."

"Do we have to pay you hush money?" asked Abigail.

"We know you're hard up," said Jacinta.

"No, don't be silly," said Friday. "I'd never dream of blackmailing you. I have principles."

"I don't," said Melanie. "You can buy my silence with that half-eaten chocolate bar on the desk."

The Headmaster's Ankle

Every Monday morning the whole school gathered for assembly, which was about as far from exciting as you can possibly get. The only interesting thing to ever happen at assembly was for someone to fall asleep, slide out of their chair, and bang their head on the floorboards, which allowed everybody one and

a half seconds to enjoy a good giggle before the Vice Principal leaped to his feet and glared them into silence.

At this particular assembly, however, something interesting had happened—the assembly hadn't started yet.

Miss Abbercroft tried to fill the time by reading the school announcements. This did not go well. The first announcement was that the escapee from the nearby maximum-security prison had still not been caught, which caused a babble of excited mutters among the students, mainly from girls wondering what they should wear in case they bumped into him.

But the second announcement was even more disturbing. The school's much-loved and extremely ancient cat, Purrcy, had passed away. He had fallen asleep on the hood of Mr. Henderson's car. Unfortunately, when Mr. Henderson started his car, he accidentally put it in reverse and rear-ended a tree, which caused a large branch to fall off and crush the cat.

"What a nice way to go," whispered Melanie. "While he was taking a nap."

But the rest of the student body did not see it that way. Many of the girls enjoyed a good hysterical weeping session and saw this as the perfect opportunity to launch into one. The announcements had to be abandoned while messengers were sent out to fetch tissues.

Friday was, of course, secretly reading a book that she had tucked inside her blazer. It was the fourth book in *The Curse of the Pirate King* series. She was just getting to a good bit where the Pirate King had his foot caught in a giant clam in rapidly rising tidal waters. Friday was curious to learn if he would cut his own foot off to escape. And if he did, she just hoped he would remember to use a tourniquet before he started cutting into his ankle with a sharpened oyster shell.

"What's going on?" asked Friday, realizing that the entire student body was sitting inside the hall while the staff milled about outside the back entrance.

"We can't begin yet," said Melanie, "because the Headmaster hasn't turned up."

"He hasn't turned up?" said Friday. "Where is he?"

"Nobody knows," said Melanie.

"Barnes!" yelled the Vice Principal from the back of the hall.

Friday flinched. Everyone turned to look at her, their eyes zeroing in on her distinctive green porkpie hat. Friday found herself wishing that an extremely localized sinkhole would open up in the floor beneath her, because, to Friday, falling into a fissure in the earth's surface would be preferable to having three hundred of her peers staring at her.

"Get out here now!" demanded the Vice Principal.

Friday took a deep breath, stood up, and began her walk of shame. She didn't even know what she was supposed to be ashamed of, so she naturally assumed the worst—that the Vice Principal had discovered something unspeakably heinous that she had no memory of doing.

"Oh dear, what have you done?" said Ian as Friday tried to squeeze past him. She could have sworn he moved his knees forward an extra inch to make it difficult.

"I'm not entirely sure," said Friday.

"Don't worry, with luck they'll just expel you," said Ian. "They won't call the police this time."

Friday ignored him as she continued to edge out of the row.

"Hello, Ian," said Melanie. She was following Friday because she suspected if she stuck close to her best friend she might be able to get out of assembly entirely.

"Good morning, Melanie," said Ian as he gallantly

got out of his seat to make it easier for her to pass and even gave a little bow.

Friday rolled her eyes and ignored him, before warily approaching the angry Vice Principal. The rest of the teaching staff was clustered in a group behind him.

"Where's the Headmaster?" demanded the Vice Principal.

"I don't know," said Friday.

"A likely story," said the Vice Principal contemptuously. "Whenever there's trouble at this school, you're always in the middle of it. You've engineered his disappearance, haven't you? No doubt with the help of your terrorist connections!"

"I don't have terrorist connections!" protested Friday.

"Well, you would say that, wouldn't you?" argued the Vice Principal.

"Yes, I would, because it's true," said Friday. "Instead of wasting time accusing me, why don't you try looking for him?"

"Of all the impertinence!" exclaimed the Vice Principal.

"I'm not being impertinent," said Friday. "I'm being

practical. I can see the whole staff is here, which tells me that none of you have had the initiative to organize a search party yet."

The teachers looked at their feet and muttered among themselves.

"You should get to it," continued Friday. "Obviously, the school grounds should be searched. But the Headmaster also likes taking early-morning walks in the forest, where he can secretly indulge his chocolate Rolo habit, so you should search there as well."

"No need," said Melanie. "Look! It's the Headmaster."

Everyone turned. In the distance they could see the Headmaster being carried up the driveway by a large vagrant.

"Who's that carrying him?" asked the Vice Principal, squinting. "Is it someone from the school?"

"It's Malcolm!" exclaimed Friday.

"Who?" asked the Vice Principal.

"He's Friday's vagrant friend," explained Melanie.

"I don't believe it!" said the shocked Vice Principal.

"Oh dear," said Friday. "I'm glad I'm not you, Vice Principal. You're going to get in trouble for this."

"But I didn't do anything!" he protested.

"Precisely," said Friday. "When the Headmaster didn't turn up, your thoughts immediately went to conspiracy theories instead of doing what a normal person would do—show concern for a missing co-worker."

"How dare you!" yelled the Vice Principal.

"Even now," said Friday, "you haven't rushed down to assist him."

The Vice Principal glared at Friday, then took off jogging down the driveway toward his employer, followed by the more athletic members of the staff.

Friday noticed that, just a few feet away, Mr. Pilcher was about to start his riding lawn mower. So instead of jogging after the teachers, she and Melanie got Mr. Pilcher to give them a ride. Friday got to the Headmaster first.

"Are you all right?" asked Friday as the mower skidded to a halt on the gravel and she was thrown off the front onto her hands and knees.

"No, I am not," snapped the Headmaster.

Now that she could look closely at him, Friday could tell that the Headmaster was in a state. He was disheveled, muddy, and sweaty, and his trousers were torn at the knees. Most significantly of all, the tube of Rolos in his pocket was unfinished, a testament to just how distressed he was that he had forgotten his chocolate friend was so close at hand.

"What happened?" asked the Vice Principal, lumbering to a panting halt. "What's he doing here?" The Vice Principal pointed at Malcolm.

"Carrying your boss," said Malcolm.

"I fell in a hole," said the Headmaster.

"Literally?" asked Melanie. "Or are you talking about a figurative or metaphoric hole?"

"No, a literal, real hole in the ground!" yelled the Headmaster. "Some vandal dug a hole right in the middle of my favorite walk."

"Like an elephant trap in a Tarzan movie," said Friday.

"Are you calling me an elephant?" demanded the Headmaster.

"No," said Friday. "I was just wondering if someone dug a hole in an attempt to trap you."

"It obviously didn't work because he's here," observed Melanie.

"The hole wasn't *that* big," said Malcolm.

"No," said Melanie, "the culprit probably gave up when he realized the enormity of the task."

"Are you saying I'm fat?" demanded the Headmaster.

"No," said Melanie, "I'm just saying if someone was to trap you in a hole, it would have to be a big hole."

"Although you are overweight," added Friday. "There's no point denying it. The waistband on your trousers is sufficient statistical evidence."

"Enough!" snapped the Headmaster. "My knees are scraped, my ankle is sprained, and my trousers are ruined. I do not want to stand here a moment longer, bandying hypothetical scenarios with the two most socially malfunctional students in the school."

"That's a bit harsh," said Friday.

"Yes, but fair, though," said Melanie.

"You need ice on that ankle," said Malcolm. "Let's get you to the infirmary." He started carrying the Headmaster toward the rear of the administration building.

"What about the assembly?" asked the Vice Principal. "Do you want me to take it for you?"

"No," barked the Headmaster. "The assembly is canceled. I want all the students to return to class, where they will each write out two hundred times 'I will not dig holes on the school grounds.'"

"What if it wasn't a student?" asked Friday. "What

if it was a member of the staff trying to get you out of the way?" She glared meaningfully at the Vice Principal.

"How dare you!" protested the Vice Principal.

"Your fingernails are dirty," observed Friday.

"Maybe he doesn't wash properly," suggested Melanie.

Friday took out her magnifying glass, ready to take a closer look.

"I was gardening," said the Vice Principal, shoving his hands in his pockets to hide just how dirty his fingernails were.

There was a thump.

"Ow!" cried the Headmaster. He lay sprawled on the ground.

"Sorry," said Malcolm. "I didn't mean to drop you. I lost my grip."

"That's quite all right," said the Headmaster. "Barnes, you can save your wild accusations for a time when I am not hobbling about in tremendous pain." The Headmaster turned to Malcolm and held out his hand. "Thank you, sir, for coming to my aid. May I repay you? Perhaps with a hot meal from our dining hall?"

"I wouldn't," said Melanie. "It's Monday. That means liverwurst sandwiches for lunch."

"I don't want to embarrass you," said the Headmaster, "but perhaps a small monetary reward . . ." He rifled in his pockets, but all he could come up with was the packet of Rolos. "Oh dear, it appears I'm the one who's embarrassed."

"I don't want anything," said Malcolm.

"But what are you still doing here?" asked Friday. "I thought you had your own place. What were you doing on school grounds?"

"I wasn't. I was across the road," said Malcolm.

"Why?" asked Friday.

"Friday," said Melanie, "you know how you like me to tell you when your rudeness levels are peaking? Well, you're definitely going up into the red zone."

"I don't have to answer your questions," said Malcolm.

"Fine, I just don't want you to get into trouble," said Friday. "Schools can be very sensitive about having an ex-criminal nearby."

"Criminal?" exclaimed the Vice Principal. "I have to notify the school council immediately!" He scurried away.

"Thanks for that," said Malcolm, glaring at Friday.

"You're welcome," said Friday with a smile.

Malcolm growled, then stomped off.

"He was being sarcastic," said Melanie.

"Really?" said Friday. "I can never pick up on that. We need a hand signal so you can let me know."

"How about I just put my hand over your mouth?" suggested Melanie.

"That would work," agreed Friday.

Chapter

11

The Mystery of the Perfect Quiche

For the next couple of weeks, life continued as normal. A rumor did go around that a mining company had infiltrated the teaching staff with a spy who was digging holes to try to find underground oil reserves. This in turn set off a craze among the students, who started digging holes on the school grounds to get to the oil reserves first, but that fad wore off when all anyone ever found was old bottle caps and the occasional ChapStick. Students gradually drifted back to their regular pursuits, which in Friday's case meant standing knee-deep in

swamp mud as she peered into a hollow log, observing moths. She was researching a paper on autumnal hibernation patterns.

"Hello!" called Rebecca Rodriguez.

Friday was concentrating so hard on the larvae that she was startled. She turned quickly, but because she was standing in thick mud, her rubber boots did not turn with her. "Oh no," said Friday as she overbalanced backward and fell into the mud, completely submerging in the thick brown slime.

"Are you all right?" asked Melanie from the safety of the wooden walkway where she was sunbathing.

"Of course I'm not

all right," said Friday as she struggled to pull herself out.

"I know," said Melanie, "but I had to say something, and I thought if I offered to help you might say yes. And I don't really want to do that."

Friday was sitting up now and trying to use a branch to pull herself to her feet.

"I'm sorry," said Rebecca as she hurried down the path to join Melanie. "I didn't mean to startle you."

"It could have happened to anyone," said Melanie. "Friday's off in a world of her own when she's observing disgusting creepy-crawlies."

Friday was laboriously wading back to the walkway. Each step produced a loud squelch as she fought the viscosity of the mud and heaved her foot forward. "I'm covered in mud," complained Friday. She was not a vain girl, but she disliked stinking like an overripe compost heap as much as the next person.

"Yes, but on the bright side," said Melanie, "the mud almost perfectly matches the color of your cardigan, so you don't have to worry about it staining."

Friday made it to the wooden walkway, and Melanie grabbed hold of the straps of her backpack to help pull her out. Rebecca Rodriguez took several steps back while Friday made her messy transition to dry land.

Neither Friday nor Melanie would have dreamed of asking Rebecca to help. She was not that kind of girl. It's not that Rebecca wasn't kind. She was just very neat and precise. As much as possible in her immediate vicinity, she liked her clothes and her hair to be perfectly clean, ironed, and arranged at all times.

Finally, Friday got to her feet. There was no point cleaning herself off. The only way she could improve her appearance would be with a high-pressure hose. She would have to ask Mr. Pilcher if she could borrow his, later.

"Now," said Friday, gathering as much composure as a mud-covered girl can manage, "how can I help you? I assume you need help. Like the vast majority of students at this school, you have never spoken to me voluntarily. And since you have sought me out—in the swamp of all places, a location that must be repugnant to someone of your fastidious nature—I must conclude that you require my professional services."

"Yes, I do," said Rebecca. "Would you mind terribly if I hold my nose while we talk?"

"Not at all," said Friday. "My clients with broken noses do it. So it would be petty of me to complain when clients of a delicate nasal nature would want to do the same."

"Judith Wilton has beaten me on the last three home economics assignments," said Rebecca.

"I see," said Friday. "But I don't understand how I can help you. Do you need tutoring?"

"I do not need coaching!" declared Rebecca, who had clearly been insulted by the inference. "I am the best home economics student at this school."

Friday wasn't sure why Rebecca would be proud of this statement. If she had gone home and told her own parents that she was the top student in home economics, they would have given her a long and exhaustive lecture, possibly using a PowerPoint presentation, on how disappointed they were that she was even studying the subject. But Friday's parents were theoretical physicists, so they thought all subjects other than physics and advanced mathematics were silly.

"If you're the best," said Friday, using reasoning cautiously, for she had discovered that the use of logical arguments could sometimes offend the girls at her school, "then why didn't you get top grades for your last three assignments?"

"I don't know!" wailed Rebecca. "I think Judith must have cheated."

"How can you cheat on a home economics assignment?" asked Friday. "Surely the proof is in the pudding—literally, if the assignment is to make a pudding."

"I don't know how she's doing it," said Rebecca. "That's why I came to you."

"Let's go back to the dorm," said Friday. "I need to clean up. We can talk as we walk."

The girls started heading up through the pathway.

"Explain from the beginning what's been going on," said Friday.

"Last term, Judith didn't do particularly well at all," said Rebecca. "Her cakes were dry and her pastries limp. She was just as bad as all the other girls. My work was always, by far, the best. I got A++ for everything."

"You can get A++ for home economics?" Friday whispered to Melanie.

Melanie just shrugged.

"But since the beginning of this term Judith's work has suddenly become brilliant," continued Rebecca. "The first week back she made a Swiss roll that was perfect."

Melanie leaned close to Friday and asked in a lowered voice, "Is she talking about rolling a Swiss citizen along the ground?"

"I don't think so," said Friday. "A Swiss roll is also a sponge cake coiled into a cylindrical shape with a jam-and-cream filling. I think it's more likely that's what she's referring to."

"Then, in week three, she made a chicken pot pie that didn't just look beautiful," said Rebecca. "It was also delectable."

"Perhaps she practiced her cooking during the summer?" suggested Friday.

"No one could improve that much," said Rebecca. "Besides, being a good cook isn't just about practice; it's about attitude, the discipline of precise measurement, and the art of combining organic products that are never exactly the same twice. You can mimic the greats by following their recipes, but you will never be great unless you have the right attitude. It has to be in your blood."

"I am gaining an increased respect for home economics," said Friday. "It is clearly a much more complicated subject than I imagined. I may take it next year. There is evidently a lot to be learned. A great deal of applied carbon chemistry, for a start."

"We've got another assignment due tomorrow," said Rebecca. "We have to make a quiche. I'm going to do my goat cheese and spinach quiche. It's mouthwatering. There's no way Judith can beat it. Not without cheating, that is."

"But surely you make all your assignments in class," said Friday. "Can't you see what she's doing as she cooks?"

"No," said Rebecca. "I sit in the front row. Judith is at the very back table. There are three workstations between us and she's directly behind me. With the other students buzzing around, I can never see what she's doing."

"What do you want me to do?" asked Friday. "I can't take off a whole double period to come and watch your home economics class."

"Just be there at the end," said Rebecca. "The finished quiches will be presented and judged by the teacher in the last ten minutes of class. That's the best time to denounce Judith and her quiche."

The Quiche-Off

At ten minutes to eleven the following morning, Friday told her ancient history teacher, Mr. Braithwaite, that she was suffering from a bout of benign positional proximal vertigo. Since Mr. Braithwaite was tired of having all his dates corrected, he gladly allowed Friday to leave the class with Melanie on the pretext of going to the nurse's office.

Friday and Melanie immediately hurried across the school, crunching through autumn leaves as they cut through the gardens to the home economics classroom.

No one noticed as Friday and Melanie slipped in the back. It was the first time Friday had been inside this classroom. There were five large benchtops with built-in stoves and hot plates. They were all littered with dirty dishes, utensils, and bowls, apart from the last bench, where the student-cook had apparently finished in such good time that she'd been able to do her dishes, which were now neatly stacked. At the other end of the classroom were big picture windows looking out on the school's impressive vegetable garden.

At the front of the room a line of eight quiches had been set out on a table, which the students gathered around. Friday could immediately see there was a large disparity in the quality of the quiches.

Six of them looked terrible. One was entirely blackened and still had globs of fire extinguisher foam on top, where it had evidently been doused. Another was wildly undercooked and had collapsed in a puddle all over the table. One was concave in the middle. Another was purple and smelled bad. One was limp and unappetizing. And another had a slimy sheen on it that almost looked like botulism. The last two, however, were an entirely different matter.

They were beautiful. Sunny and golden on top. High and deep with a crisp pastry casing. The vegetables coyly poked out of the eggy filling.

The teacher, Mrs. Piccone, had passed judgment on the first six quiches and was standing in front of the final perfect two.

"Rebecca and Judith," said the teacher. "Well done, girls. You've done a lovely job."

Friday and Melanie edged closer to get a better look. The teacher was inspecting the two quiches very closely. Friday inspected the two girls. Rebecca looked her normal immaculate self, not a hair out of place, her apron spotlessly clean. But her face looked anxious. She wanted this. She wanted to win very badly.

Judith, on the other hand, was the polar opposite. She looked a mess. Her hair was ruffled, and there was flour all over her apron, her hands, on top of her hair, and even the middle of her back. And she looked happy, like she was pleased to have made such a lovely quiche and had enjoyed the process.

Mrs. Piccone carefully cut into Rebecca's quiche. "Good texture," she said, placing a slice on a plate.

"Excellent color on the inside." It looked lovely, the green spinach and white goat cheese all in cross-section. Mrs. Piccone took out a spoon, scooped up a mouthful, and tasted it. "Mmm," she said. "Nice balance of vegetable and cheese. Good spring in the egg mix. Perhaps . . . could do with a tad more salt, though."

Rebecca looked crushed. She hung her head and nodded, taking the criticism on board.

Next, Mrs. Piccone cut a slice of Judith's quiche and laid it on a plate. It was gorgeous. Spears of bright green asparagus interlaced the egg mix. "Stunning!" said Mrs. Piccone.

Judith beamed with pleasure. The other girls smiled and congratulated her. Except for Rebecca. She just looked pale.

Mrs. Piccone tasted a mouthful of Judith's quiche. "Mmm, oh my goodness," she said. "That is fabulous. What an intriguing blend of flavors. The egg mixture complements the vegetables perfectly. What is that condiment you used?" Mrs. Piccone tried another mouthful. "Is it truffle oil?"

Judith nodded. "Yes, ma'am."

"How did you get the idea to make this wonderful combination of flavors?" asked Mrs. Piccone.

"I was inspired by the garden," said Judith, indicating the school's extensive vegetable patch beyond the window. "I wanted everything to be fresh. I picked the asparagus this morning."

"An inspiration!" said Mrs. Piccone, putting another and even larger spoonful into her mouth. "Girls, you should all try this. You could learn a lot by following Judith's example."

"Not so fast!" declared Friday. "The only thing these girls can learn from Judith is how to be a cheat."

"Excuse me! Who are you?" asked Mrs. Piccone. "And what are you doing here?"

"My name is Friday Barnes," said Friday, "and I am here to investigate the suspiciously brilliant cooking of your student Judith Wilton."

"You're pathetic," said Judith, turning on Rebecca. "You can't handle being second best, so you hired a detective."

"Rebecca may well have an unhealthy and irrational desire to be better than everyone else at cooking," agreed Friday, "but in this instance she was entirely justified in her suspicions."

"Ma'am," said Judith to Mrs. Piccone, "Friday needs to go to the infirmary. Her brain has become unhinged."

The other girls sniggered.

"Girls," snapped Mrs. Piccone, "you know making mean comments about another person's mental health is against school rules."

"I'm only trying to help her, ma'am," protested Judith. "Just look at her clothes. She clearly doesn't fit in here—or anywhere outside of a charity clothing bin. That brown cardigan is a cry for help."

"I wish I'd brought a voice recorder," said Friday, turning to Melanie. "Judith is putting on an impressive display of teenage verbal intimidation clichés."

"You mean she's being a bully?" asked Melanie.

"I wouldn't use such a crude term," said Friday, "no matter how accurate. But her abuse is enlightening. It is a typical behavioral response to lash out and attempt to demean your accuser when you've been caught cheating."

"What are you talking about?" asked Mrs. Piccone. "There is no way anyone can cheat in home economics. The students have to make their quiche right here in class, where they can be seen at all times."

"Improbable but not impossible," said Friday. "Certainly not if the entire class was in on the charade."

"What?!" exclaimed Mrs. Piccone.

"I believe the entire class conspired to beat Rebecca at quiche making," said Friday.

"But that's delusional," said Mrs. Piccone.

Friday eyed the entire class. They looked unusually smug for a group in which all but one had failed disastrously.

"I know," agreed Friday. "But there is no one more petty and delusional than a teenage girl. And when you get a whole group of them together, their pettiness and delusion combine to form hysteria. And once teenage girls whip themselves up into a hysterical frenzy, they are capable of any merciless act. The Salem witch trials are a prime example."

"Miss, she's bullying me," complained Judith. "I want to call my father, to have him consult our lawyer."

"Nobody will be consulting their lawyer," said Mrs. Piccone. "This whole thing is ridiculous; there is no evidence to support your wild accusation at all."

"On the contrary," said Friday. "I have three pieces of evidence, and I am sure when I investigate I shall find more."

"You're going to be finished at this school after this," said Judith. "No one will ever talk to you again.

"Nobody much talks to her now," said Melanie.

"You do," said Friday.

"Yes," said Melanie, "but I'm your best friend. Besides, no one talks to me either. If I didn't talk to you, I'd have to go back to talking to the wall, which is always a very one-sided conversation."

"Just tell us your evidence and get on with it," said Mrs. Piccone.

"I draw your attention to Judith's hair," said Friday. "You will see there is flour all through it."

"So? The girls made the crusts from scratch," said Mrs. Piccone. "They had to use flour."

"Not all of us are clean freaks like Rebecca," said Judith.

The other girls giggled again.

"I can see how an unfastidious person could get flour on their apron, and even on their face and the hair around their face during the cooking process," agreed Friday. "But I cannot see how you would get flour on the top of your head and the middle of your back, unless you or someone else deliberately put it there."

"Why would she do that?" asked Mrs. Piccone.

"To make it look like she had been cooking," said Friday, "when she had not been. She had merely reheated a quiche she had brought from home."

"That's absurd," said Judith.

"Then there are her dishes," said Friday. "If you look to the back bench where Judith works, you will see that her dishes are clean, whereas everyone else's dishes still have congealing egg mixture or pastry dough crusting on."

"So I did my dishes," said Judith. "There's nothing wrong with that."

"You can't have done your dishes, because your hands are still covered in flour," said Friday. "Even if you wore rubber gloves, the flour would have rubbed off. Your dishes are clean because they were never dirty in the first place."

"It's all just circumstantial evidence," said Stacey. She was Judith's best friend and her father was doing five to ten for insurance fraud, so she was able to use big words like "circumstantial evidence" accurately in a sentence.

"Yes, perhaps," agreed Friday. "But there is no explanation for Judith's lie."

"What are you talking about?" asked Judith.

"You said you picked the vegetables for your quiche by hand this morning," said Friday. "But there is asparagus in your quiche, and asparagus is a spring vegetable. It won't be ready in the garden for another six months."

"That's not true," protested Judith.

"It can be easily checked," said Friday. "If you all look out the window, you will see the asparagus patch at the far end of the garden. It is the big patch of dirt with nothing growing in it."

"So I used canned asparagus," said Judith.

Friday shook her head. "You are digging yourself into a deeper hole, revealing how little you really know about cooking. Before it is canned, asparagus is cooked and stored in brine, which has a significant effect on its texture and color."

"Canned asparagus doesn't look like fresh asparagus," said Rebecca. "It is soft and smaller and a grayish yellow tinge in color."

"This is a terrible allegation," said Mrs. Piccone.

"Yes, we shall need some supporting evidence," agreed Friday, "but now that we have a working theory, let us extrapolate. Mrs. Piccone, what is the next cooking assignment for this class?"

"We are going to make apple pie next week," said Mrs. Piccone.

"And your students are aware of the assignment schedule ahead of time, I presume?" asked Friday.

"Why, yes," said Mrs. Piccone. "I give them a list before the fall break so they can practice."

"So if Judith brought a stash of premade baked goods from home at the beginning of the term, where would she have hidden them?" asked Friday.

"They'd have to be frozen," said Melanie. "So, I guess, in a freezer?"

"Good deductive reasoning, Melanie," said Friday. "You're improving."

"Thank you," said Melanie. She so rarely listened to conversations, it was nice to have the extra effort pay off.

"Shall we check the deep freezer?" Friday asked Mrs. Piccone.

"It's over here," said Mrs. Piccone, leading Friday to the corner of the classroom.

Friday opened the lid of the enormous chest freezer and saw that it was full of plastic bags containing vegetables, stocks of various flavors, sauces, and cuts of meat. She took the packages out, one by one, and laid them on the floor.

"She's letting the food ruin, ma'am," complained Stacey.

"Stop complaining," said Mrs. Piccone. "If you absorbed any of the information I taught you about home economics, you'd know it would take a leg of lamb more than a few seconds to thaw."

Friday kept digging. "Aha!" She had bent over so far she practically tumbled headfirst into the freezer. Friday grabbed something from the bottom and pulled herself upright. She was holding a large white cardboard box. The box had a handwritten message on the lid:

PURRCY
(DEAD CAT)

"Don't open that," warned Mrs. Piccone. "That's Purrcy, the school cat. We're storing him here until the end of the term, when Mrs. Henderson is taking him back to her home to bury him in her sandpit. Purrcy loved a sandpit."

"Really?" said Friday. "Do you believe in reincarnation, Mrs. Piccone?"

"No," said Mrs. Piccone.

"Then how do you explain Purrcy's transformation into an apple pie?" Friday opened the box and revealed a perfect-looking apple pie.

Mrs. Piccone gasped. All the girls looked guilty except for Rebecca, who looked angry and smug all at the same time.

"I think if you call Judith's home you will soon discover a maid, a cook, or some other member of the domestic staff who will confess to making this dessert," said Friday.

"Girls, I don't understand," said Mrs. Piccone. "How could you? Why would you?"

"We were so sick of Rebecca's smirking superiority," said Judith. "We just did it as a joke, really."

"Yeah, that's right," agreed Stacey. The other girls nodded as well. "It's a joke. Just like Rebecca is a joke."

Rebecca looked hurt.

"You should make sure you enjoy every last moment of high school, then," said Friday. "It is the last place you'll find where a person is scorned for caring about what they do and working hard to be good at it. Rebecca may well be an obsessive freak, but in the real world she has all the makings of a top-class gourmet chef, once she learns to swear like a sailor, that is."

"Home economics has always been a subject rife with vitriolic rivalries," said Mrs. Piccone. "But bringing a dead cat into it? That is a new low. You are all going to have to go and see the Headmaster."

"Poor Headmaster," said Melanie. "He's going to need a bigger bench."

"There's one more mystery that needs to be settled first," said Friday. "What did you do with Purrcy's body?"

"We buried him in the rose garden outside the Headmaster's office," said Judith.

"At least that's a suitable, respectful resting place," said Friday, unexpectedly impressed by the thoughtfulness of the girls.

"We found a hole there, so we thought that would do the job," said Stacey. "Save us having to dig one up ourselves."

Rebecca shook her head sadly. "You see, it is this slipshod mentality that will prevent them from ever becoming good cooks."

A Secret in the Woods

It was mandatory for students at High-crest Academy to join at least one extra-curricular club. Friday had pointed out to the Headmaster that by making an activity compulsory, it therefore was no longer extracurricular, but rather just curricular. The Head-master simply told her to be quiet and go back to class.

Naturally the first club Friday had joined was the science club. It was run by one of Friday's favorite teachers, Mr. Davies. There was very little he could teach Friday that she didn't already know. But what she liked about Mr. Davies was his enthusiasm. The delight he took in explaining the process of osmosis, the genuine wonder with which he held the periodic table, and the excitement he felt for Newtonian physics were all contagious. For Mr. Davies, every day spent exploring science was as fun as a day at Disneyland, something Mr. Davies also highly recommended, because there is no better place to study gravity, momentum, and centrifugal force than in the loop-de-loop of a roller coaster.

The science club had spent the previous two weeks observing oral bacteria by spitting into petri dishes and then watching what grew. It was a disgusting but educational exercise. This week's meeting was promising to be even more exciting. They were going to explore aeronautical physics by building rockets. The student whose rocket flew the highest would get a bar of chocolate.

Friday was pouring all her knowledge of physics (which was considerable after growing up in a house with six physicists) into building the most aerodynamically pure and chemically potent rocket she possibly could. Melanie helped, of course. It was her job to sit at the desk so that she blocked Ian's view of what Friday was doing.

"Are we all ready?" asked Mr. Davies. He was holding his own bright red rocket, which was about the size of a mailing tube and had flickering flames painted on the side. He was practically dancing from foot to foot with excitement. "Then let's go."

The students got up from their desks and made their way with their rockets to the door. The rockets were going to be fired from the school baseball field. A vertical measure had been erected, and a high-speed camera was being used so that the flights could be accurately gauged.

"I don't know why you're bothering, Barnes," said Ian as the bottleneck of the doorway drew him and Friday together. "This is a real practical experiment, not a hypothetical mind game like you usually play."

"I'm perfectly capable of transferring my intellectual knowledge to real-world scenarios," said Friday.

"Really?" said Ian. "But you apparently can't manage the simple real-world task of tying your shoelaces."

Friday looked down. "What are you talking about?" she asked. "They're tied."

"Yes, but you doubted yourself enough that you had

to check, didn't you?" said Ian. "Let's see if you have the same faith in your rocket."

"Oooh," said Melanie. "You should write down some of this witty banter so you can read the transcripts to your grandchildren one day."

"I didn't know Barnes and Wainscott were planning to start a family," said Christopher.

Friday blushed. She didn't realize that Christopher was standing close by.

"Oh yes," said Melanie, "it's inevitable. They're just in denial because neither of them is very in touch with their emotions."

"Melanie," said Friday.

"Don't worry, your secret is safe with me," said Christopher with a wink.

"I'm not marrying anyone," protested Friday.

"Don't be so hard on yourself," said Melanie. "Sure, you are a little odd, but you can be pretty when you're not wearing your green hat and brown cardigan. Ian won't be able to resist you forever."

Mercifully, thoughts of romance were soon forgotten when the students found themselves standing in the middle of a cold, damp field, waiting for their turn to fire their rockets. Mr. Davies had lined them up in a row and was personally supervising each launch. It was actually not as exciting as you might imagine, because there is a lot that can go wrong with a rocket: electrical faults, design failures, damp in the connectors. The first two rockets didn't fire at all, which made the girls who built them giggle. They'd only joined the science club because word had gotten out that Christopher, the dreamy new boy, had signed up.

The third rocket did fire, but then it spun in tight circles, never making it more than six feet off the ground before embedding itself nose-first in the baseball field.

"Oh dear, Mr. Pilcher isn't going to be happy about that," worried Mr. Davies. "He's already got enough holes to deal with."

Then it was Ian's turn. Friday and Melanie took a couple of steps back, just in case Ian had packed his rocket with chocolate pudding or some other prank. Ian nonchalantly held the launch button in his hand.

"When you're ready, Mr. Wainscott," said Mr. Davies.

Ian smiled his smug smile, which made the girls giggle again. "Can I have a countdown, ladies?" he asked.

The girls giggled some more. Friday rolled her eyes. "This will be interesting. I wonder if they can count backward from ten."

Evidently the girls did not like to stretch themselves, because they started from five. "Five . . . four . . . three . . . two . . . one . . . Blast off!"

Ian pressed the launch button and . . . nothing happened. His face fell. He started to walk toward the rocket to see what the problem was.

Friday instinctively did the same. Ian might be her nemesis, but she never enjoyed seeing an experiment fail. They both arrived at the rocket at the same moment, when suddenly—*WHOOOSH*—the rocket shot up in the air. Friday stumbled backward and landed on her bottom. She looked up to see the rocket high in the sky.

"Two-fifty, two-seventy-five, three hundred feet!" came a crackly voice over Mr. Davies's walkie-talkie. There was an observer standing on the roof of the administration building.

"Well done, Wainscott!" said Mr. Davies, applauding enthusiastically.

Ian smiled down at Friday. "Do you think you can beat that?"

"We'll see," said Friday.

"Christopher Gianos, you're up next," said Mr. Davies.

Christopher stepped forward, made a couple of last-minute adjustments to his rocket, and then stood back. He looked a little nervous.

"Would you like us to count down for you, too?" tittered Mirabella.

"No, thank you, I prefer to create dramatic tension in my own way," said Christopher. He turned and looked at Ian. "By saying kiss . . . my . . ."

WHOOOSH!

Christopher's rocket took off. Right away it was evident his rocket was going at a greater speed than Ian's.

"Two hundred . . . two-fifty . . ." said the voice over the walkie-talkie.

"Well done, Gianos!" exclaimed Mr. Davies.

"Three hundred . . . three-twenty-five!" continued the voice on the radio.

Christopher smiled and cocked his head at Ian, who glowered. The rocket was still going.

"Four hundred, five hundred . . . six hundred feet!" concluded the voice on the walkie-talkie.

"That's a new school record!" exclaimed Mr. Davies.

"I've never gotten a rocket above five-fifty myself. You'll have to take me through your exact construction process." Mr. Davies slapped Christopher on the back and shook his hand.

"There's still one more to go," said Ian.

"What?" asked Mr. Davies.

"Friday's," said Ian.

"Oh yes, Barnes," said Mr. Davies. "Of course, didn't see you there. Must be that brown cardigan. Go ahead, you have your turn."

Friday picked up her launch button.

"I'm sure Mirabella will do a countdown for you if you ask her nicely," said Ian.

"I wouldn't want to strain her mathematical skills," said Friday. "Melanie, will you do the honors?"

"Sorry, what?" said Melanie. "I wasn't paying attention."

"Never mind," said Friday. "I'm sorry to have interrupted your daydream."

"That's quite all right," said Melanie, staring off into the middle distance again.

"I'll do it myself," said Friday. "Ready . . . aim . . . fire!"

Friday pressed her button and the whole launchpad

exploded in a *BOOM!* The rocket shot upwards, but it sounded different from Christopher's and Ian's, more of a roar than a whoosh.

"One-fifty . . . two hundred . . . two-fifty . . ." said the voice over the walkie-talkie, but then Friday's rocket seemed to slow. "Two-seventy-five . . .

"Hard luck, Barnes," said Ian, smug once more.

"Wait for it," said Friday.

BOOM! The rocket exploded midair, or rather the tail section did, and the nose section took off again even faster.

"What was that?!" asked Mr. Davies.

"The secondary booster," explained Friday.

"Genius!" exclaimed Mr. Davies, watching the rocket through his binoculars.

"I know," agreed Friday.

"Six-fifty . . ." said the voice over the walkie-talkie. "One thousand . . . one thousand five hundred . . . It's too high, I can't measure it anymore."

"That's all right," said Friday, "I can." She reached into her backpack and pulled out a handheld electronic device.

"That's cheating!" exclaimed Ian. "Electronics are against school rules."

"Not all electronics," said Friday. "The school rules specifically state which electronic devices are not allowed, and there is no mention of three-dimensional GPS trackers. Two thousand five hundred feet."

"No way!" exclaimed Christopher.

"NASA satellites don't lie," said Friday.

"Bravo, Miss Barnes," said Mr. Davies.

"Four thousand feet . . . five thousand feet . . . six thousand feet . . . six thousand one hundred ninety-seven feet!" declared Friday. "That's the zenith, it's coming down."

High above them they could see a parachute pop out from the tail section. The rocket slowed to a gentle downward drift.

"Congratulations, Miss Barnes!" said Mr. Davies, shaking Friday by the hand.

"It must be windy up there," said Melanie, shading her eyes as she kept watching the rocket. "It's being blown sideways."

"What?" said Friday, looking up again. "Uh-oh, we should have sent up a weather balloon first so we could measure wind speed at the various heights."

The rocket was drifting on the wind toward the south.

"You'll be lucky if it lands on school grounds," said Ian.

"I don't think it will," said Christopher.

They all watched the parachute drift over the school boundary, still a thousand feet in the air and floating rapidly away from them.

"Oh dear, oh dear," said Mr. Davies. "How are we going to get it back? I'll get in such trouble with the Headmaster if I lose any more equipment. He's still angry with me for blowing up the fume hood last semester when I got carried away demonstrating a baking-powder volcano."

"That's all right," said Friday, "it'll be simple to find with the GPS."

"Are you sure?" asked Mr. Davies.

"I've even got video footage," said Friday.

"You do?" asked Mr. Davies.

Friday took a tablet computer out of her bag.

"Now that is definitely against the school rules," said Ian.

"I'm sure Mr. Davies and the Headmaster will be happy to bend the rules if it means I can return the school's equipment," said Friday.

"Oh yes, of course, of course," said Mr. Davies.

"I embedded a nanocamera in the rocket's nose cone," said Friday, tapping the screen on her tablet. "So let's see what it got."

Everyone gathered around to see the recording. Friday hit the Play arrow. For several seconds the footage was just blue sky.

"Thrilling," said Ian sarcastically.

But then the picture tipped over and they could see the school from five thousand feet up.

"Wow!" exclaimed Mr. Davies.

It really was a beautiful scene. For the students at Highcrest it was so easy to focus on the drudgery and pettiness of everyday life at a boarding school, and to forget how beautiful their school grounds were. The red stone buildings, the green ball fields all set between the winding river, the canopy of the swamp on one side and the dense forest on the other.

They watched the school gradually leave the camera's frame as the rocket drifted toward the forest, the picture getting closer and closer to the treetops. Then the rocket dipped down into the foliage.

"I hope it doesn't get stuck on a branch," worried Friday.

But the rocket didn't. The picture drifted down until

the nose hit the grass, then the rocket fell sideways, leaving a camera view of the ground through the thin grass.

"Now that's helpful," said Ian. "I'd recognize that blade of grass anywhere."

"Is that a trailer home behind the tree in the background?" asked Melanie.

Friday leaned in to peer closely at the picture. "I think you're right. Someone must be living in the forest," she said.

Suddenly a face appeared sideways in the picture.

"Aaaagggh!!!" screamed the assembled group.

Friday dropped the computer as she instinctively flinched away, but she quickly picked it back up again. The face was still sideways, but it filled up the full frame.

"It looks like a vagrant," said Mr. Davies.

"Yes," agreed Friday. "And that vagrant looks very familiar."

The Familiar Vagrant

Hello, Malcolm, good to see you again," said Friday cheerily as she arrived at the precise GPS coordinates in the woods where her rocket said it would be. Ian and Melanie were with her, Melanie because she went everywhere with Friday and Ian because Mr. Davies insisted that they needed a chaperone.

Malcolm was standing in front of a small trailer home that was tucked underneath the broad branches of an oak tree. There was a picnic chair and a card table set up outside. It looked almost homey.

"What are you doing here?" demanded Malcolm.

"We're here for the rocket," said Friday.

"Why did you fire it at me?" asked Malcolm.

"Fire it at you?" said Friday. "We didn't fire it at you. We fired it up in the air and the wind carried it here."

"You expect me to believe that?" accused Malcolm.

"Well, I would expect you to because it's the truth," said Friday. "But I don't really mind if you don't believe me, as long as you give the rocket back." She held out her hand and smiled at Malcolm. But he was still looking suspicious.

"There's a tiny camera in this thing, isn't there?" said Malcolm.

"Yes," said Friday happily. "We got some tremendous pictures of the landscape. Would you like to see the video?"

"No, I wouldn't," growled Malcolm. "I don't want you spying on me."

"We weren't," said Friday.

"I know Highcrest Academy wants to get rid of me," said Malcolm.

"They do?" said Friday.

"They wrote me a letter," said Malcolm.

"But you don't have a mailbox," said Melanie, looking around to see if there was a mailbox she had missed.

"It was hand-delivered by the Vice Principal," said Malcolm.

"Are you sure?" asked Melanie. "Our Headmaster is a wonderful man, but being on top of things is not a strength of his. If he did know you were here, he'd probably pretend he didn't so that he wouldn't have to do anything."

"Just get out of here," said Malcolm.

"Okay," said Friday. For the first time since she'd met Malcolm at the police station, Friday became conscious of his menacing size. "Can I have my rocket back, please?"

Malcolm glared. "No."

"But I got you off the hook for the theft of the sapphire bracelet," said Friday. "You owe me a favor."

"Do I?" said Malcolm. "I never understood why you helped me in the first place. Maybe you had your own reasons. Now get off my land."

"Your land?" said Friday.

"Yes, my grandfather left me this land," said Malcolm. "I own it, and you're trespassing."

Ian grabbed Friday's arm. "Come on, let's go. We don't want trouble."

Friday looked at Malcolm. He looked upset. It couldn't be easy getting let out of prison. And having a rocket unexpectedly plummet out of the sky would be alarming.

"All right," said Friday. "Sorry that we upset you. Maybe we'll bump into each other again sometime and we can explain things properly."

"Just leave me alone!" yelled Malcolm.

"Nice to meet you," said Melanie with a wave as the three students left the clearing. "What a lovely man."

"Are you kidding me?" said Ian. "He looked like he was about to explode."

"Yes," agreed Melanie. "But if you looked past that he had lovely soft eyes."

"Come on, let's get moving," said Ian, hastening his stride. "I'll feel better once we're back on school grounds."

"Wait up," said Friday. "Some of us have shorter legs than you."

Ian turned his head to say something sarcastic. "Some of us have—"

"Watch out for the hole," warned Melanie.

"Wha . . . Aagghhh!" said Ian as he stepped forward into a hole and fell over.

The girls hurried to him.

"Are you all right?" asked Friday.

"Urgh," groaned Ian.

"For an athletic boy, he gets surprisingly clumsy when he is around you," Melanie observed.

"Another hole," said Friday, bending down to look at

the neat way the hole had been cut into the ground with a sharp spade.

"Perhaps Malcolm dug it?" suggested Melanie. "Maybe he's planning to plant potatoes."

"Ian looks concussed," said Friday. "We're going to have to help him get back to the school."

Friday and Melanie pulled Ian to his feet. He was very groggy. The girls each took one of his arms around their shoulders and began slowly walking him toward the main road.

"He's very heavy," said Melanie.

"Yes," agreed Friday. "And being tall, he's got an awkwardly high center of gravity."

"It's a shame you couldn't have fallen in love with someone smaller," said Melanie. "Like Christopher."

"I'm not attracted to Christopher!" said Friday.

"I didn't say you were," said Melanie. "I just meant he was shorter. Although it is interesting that your mind leaped to that conclusion."

Mrs. Cannon's Assignment

"Class, you have no idea how much it grieves me to do this," said Mrs. Cannon as she sat at her desk, the newspaper for once folded and lying unread. "But I'm afraid the school forces me to give you an assignment."

"That's all right, ma'am," called Peregrine. "We know you've got no say in it."

"I'm totally against assignments on principle," continued Mrs. Cannon. "It's bad enough that you have to do them. But think about me. I have to grade them. All of them. And there are so many of you. It's really very exhausting."

"Is there any way we can make it easier for you?" asked Ian.

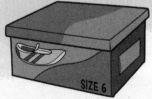

SIZE 6

"No, it's all right," said Mrs. Cannon. "Fortunately I've been doing this job for a very long time, so I am very good at coming up with assignments that involve the least amount of work for everyone."

"You're a credit to your profession, ma'am," said Ian.

"I know," said Mrs. Cannon. "Several decades ago I came up with the brilliant idea of making the fall semester assignment a time capsule."

"A time capsule?!" the class exclaimed.

"The idea is that you, as a group, put together a literary collection," said Mrs. Cannon. "It can include books or passages from a book or poems. Whatever you like. As long as it's small enough to fit in a shoebox. We don't have any earth-moving equipment, so we don't want to commit to anything too labor-intensive. The idea is that we can share a snapshot of our literary epoch with future generations."

"Sounds very worthy, ma'am," chimed in Amelia.

"I know. I was particularly proud when I came up with that phrase," reminisced Mrs. Cannon. "But the best thing about this assignment is that it is buried deep in the ground, so no one will ever know what we put in there. And no grading for me!"

"How will we get our grades?" asked Lindy, a bookish girl.

"I'll put a list of your names up on the wall and you can write in what grade you want," said Mrs. Cannon.

There was excited muttering now.

"But be warned," said Mrs. Cannon. "I know it is tempting to nominate an A. But if you've never had an A before in English and you think you're unlikely to get an A ever again, then it's best not to raise your parents' expectations. If your performance leaps up, they'll probably think you've cheated. Or if they're naïve enough to think you've suddenly become smarter, they'll be bitterly disappointed with every grade you ever get in the future. So my advice is, look into your heart and write down what you think you'd really get if you had a more professional teacher. And don't do anything silly that will draw attention to my system, because next semester I'm planning to assess you by getting you to write one haiku each. There are only seventeen syllables in a haiku. Don't make the head of English notice what I'm up to and force me to force you to write something longer."

"So when do we have to have our time capsule submissions ready?" asked Friday.

"Tomorrow," said Mrs. Cannon.

"But that only gives us twenty-three hours to think of something," said Friday.

"That's twenty-two and a half hours more than you need," said Mrs. Cannon. "Just bring in some piece of writing you'd like to bury in the ground forever."

Friday's English class gathered again for third period the following morning.

"All righty then," said Mrs. Cannon as she plonked an empty shoebox on her desk. "I suppose we'd better get this over with. What have you got?"

The students laid out their time capsule offerings.

"What's this?" asked Mrs. Cannon, picking up a comic book. "Who put this here?"

"I did, ma'am," said Rajiv. "It's a Spider-Man comic."

"Did you enjoy reading it?" asked Mrs. Cannon.

"Er . . . yes, ma'am," admitted Rajiv.

"Then don't put it in," said Mrs. Cannon. "Anything that goes in the time capsule will never be seen again. It would be a shame to waste something as enjoyable as a good comic."

"But what about the future generations?" asked Rajiv.

"They might not have an appreciation for literature,

in which case it will be wasted on them," said Mrs. Cannon. "You're better off giving it to a small child or, better yet, keeping it for yourself." She handed the comic back to Rajiv, who looked relieved to be able to tuck it inside his jacket pocket.

"What's this?" asked Mrs. Cannon, holding up a thick novel.

"*Les Misérables*," said Melanie.

"I can see that," said Mrs. Cannon. "Why on earth are you putting it in here?"

"It's painfully boring, ma'am," said Melanie.

"That's true enough," agreed Mrs. Cannon. "There are good bits in there, eventually. But you have to wade through so much blather before you get to the love triangles and the barricades. You're much better off going to see the musical. But you can't put the book in the time capsule—there's not enough space."

"What if you burned it first?" asked Melanie. "Ashes would take up less room."

"Good point," said Mrs. Cannon. "I like your lateral thinking. Be sure to give yourself an A for this assignment."

"Plus, if it's ashes, the people digging it up will assume you're making some sort of poetic statement, perhaps about the death of literature," suggested Friday.

"I like that," said Mrs. Cannon.

"Perhaps we should burn all our contributions," said Ian.

Mrs. Cannon gave Ian a scathing look. "You just want to play with matches. And as we all know, naughty boys should never play with matches."

"You're so right, ma'am," agreed Ian.

"What are you putting in, Friday?" asked Peregrine.

"I'm prepared to excuse you if you haven't got a book or poem you can bear to part with," said Mrs. Cannon.

"I'm putting in my copy of *Men Are from Mars, Women Are from Venus*," said Friday.

"Really?" said Mrs. Cannon. "I thought that was a thoroughly good book. It certainly helped me in my relationship with Mr. Cannon. Once I understood that he wanted to be left alone in his man cave, it allowed me much more time for novel reading."

"I think it's good, too," said Friday. "I like how it simplistically and with no scientific evidence undermines the entire premise of feminism—that the two genders are equal—and promotes hugging as a universal solution to the entire female gender."

"I like hugging," said Melanie.

"Women do," said Friday. "That is the genius of the book."

Ian shoved a book into the shoebox.

"What's this, Mr. Wainscott?" asked Mrs. Cannon, picking up his contribution and reading the cover. "*The Curse of the Pirate King*? This is our class reading for the semester! Are you making some sort of criticism of my curriculum?"

"No, ma'am," said Ian, looking down at his shoes as he scuffed at the floor.

"If it were, you'd get an A," said Mrs. Cannon happily. "Burying your required reading text is a very poetic way to criticize the book. Well done!" Mrs. Cannon looked at the back cover. "And I see it is a copy from the school library. Even better! That will infuriate the librarian. But technically it won't be leaving school grounds, so there won't be much she can do about it. An A+ for you, too, Mr. Wainscott."

"Come on," said Ian. "Let's bury the time capsule so we can get back to something more meaningful, like helping Mrs. Cannon with her crossword." He scooped up the box.

"You're such an angry young man," said Mrs. Cannon as she allowed a student to help her to her feet. "But so good-looking. You can get away with anything if you're beautiful. I know it's hard to believe, but I was beautiful once."

"You still are, ma'am," said Ian chivalrously.

"Good one, Mr. Wainscott," said Mrs. Cannon with a chuckle. "But seriously, I was stunning for twenty-three years, from my midteens to my late thirties. I highly recommend it. It was a lot of fun."

"Why did you stop being good-looking?" asked Melanie. "Was it age?"

"Oh no," said Mrs. Cannon. "I married Mr. Cannon. He's a chef, you know. I very quickly got fat. Which was even more fun."

The class wandered out onto the school grounds, looking for an appropriate place to bury the time capsule.

"Let's not walk too far," said Mrs. Cannon. "Where would be a good spot for the hole?"

"Right here?" suggested Melanie.

"We're standing on blacktop," Friday pointed out. "If we had a jackhammer, maybe. But we've only got the spade Mrs. Cannon brought from home."

"If we're going for maximum laziness," said Ian, "we should bury it in the school vegetable garden. The soil there gets dug over all the time. It will be the easiest place to dig a hole."

"I like your thinking, Mr. Wainscott," said Mrs. Cannon. "Make sure you give yourself an A++ for this assignment. You've earned it."

And so the class ambled in the direction of the vegetable garden.

"If a member of the staff comes near us," said Mrs. Cannon, "start discussing books so they don't suspect that we're just wandering around in the sunshine."

"But we *are* just wandering around in the sunshine," said Peregrine.

"We can't let word get out that we're doing that," said Mrs. Cannon. "Nature walks aren't part of the curriculum. At least not part of the English curriculum. Mr. Powell could probably justify doing it as part of PE, if PE teachers weren't all sadists."

When they arrived at the vegetable garden, it was agreed by consensus that the best place to dig a hole would be the brussels sprouts patch because no one liked brussels sprouts, so no one would likely dig there.

"Okay, the next question is, Who is going to dig the hole?" asked Mrs. Cannon. "Has anyone here ever used a spade before?"

Friday was the only person in the class who put up their hand.

"Really, Miss Barnes? I'm impressed. You wouldn't have struck me as the earth-moving type," said Mrs. Cannon.

"One summer I did a transactional study of the insect life in our back garden," explained Friday.

"Then the job is yours," said Mrs. Cannon, handing her the spade.

Watching Friday dig was quite a sight to behold. True, she had done it before, but she had also run before and she was still really bad at that. Doing a

physical activity that required the use of a large, heavy implement was never going to look pretty.

To start with, she was too short for the spade. Then she had almost no upper-body strength with which to swing it. And finally, when Friday did get the point of the blade into the ground, she wasn't heavy enough to force it farther into the dirt. She just stood on the shoulders of the spade and wobbled.

The class watched her for several minutes. Some giggled, but most just stood around, bored. Finally, Friday scraped a hole deep enough and the shoebox was placed inside and Friday refilled it.

"Excellent," said Mrs. Cannon. "Now that's sorted, we just have to mark it on the map."

"What map?" asked Friday.

"I've been doing this assignment for forty years," said Mrs. Cannon. "I have a map in the school library's archives with all the time capsules marked on it."

"You're not a fan of updating your lesson plan, are you, ma'am?" said Ian.

"Why would I when it's such a good one?" said Mrs. Cannon. "Now let's go to the library."

"Ah, that might be a problem," said Friday. "I'm banned from the library."

"Really?" said Mrs. Cannon. "What did you do?"

"I told the librarian she should be ashamed of her molecular biology section and that the excessive representation of nineteenth-century romance literature in the school's collection was a sad reflection of her own personal reading tastes," said Friday.

"And she didn't take that well?" asked Mrs. Cannon.

"No," admitted Friday. "I'm afraid that coming from an academic background, I often forget that some people do not enjoy enthusiastic and detailed constructive criticism."

"You hurt her feelings," said Melanie.

"Apparently so," said Friday. "She cut up my library card and put my picture behind the desk with a sign saying I was not allowed admittance to the library, even if it was raining."

"Harsh punishment for someone who actually likes reading books," observed Mrs. Cannon.

"Yes," agreed Friday.

"Well, this is going to be fun," said Mrs. Cannon. "The only thing I enjoy almost as much as doing nothing is doing something to make the librarian squirm."

At the Library

Mrs. Cannon and her English class pushed open the heavy green double doors leading into the library.

Inside, it was completely quiet. There wasn't a person to be seen. Except for Chen, the library monitor, who was standing at the circulation desk stamping books in silence. Friday wondered if the stamp was made of some sort of special rubber polymer that absorbed sound. As Friday's foot crossed the threshold, a silent alarm must have been tripped, because the librarian glided out of her office.

"Hello," said the librarian in a soft voice, which was just quiet enough to be slightly hard to hear.

"Hello, Marjorie. We're here to look at the map," said Mrs. Cannon loudly. "You're looking wan today. You should get out and enjoy the sunshine. We've just been digging in the vegetable garden."

"I hope you're not going to trek dirt in here," said the librarian.

"Would you like us to leave our shoes outside?" asked Mrs. Cannon.

"No, I would not," said the librarian. "I do not find the sweaty feet of children to be preferable. At least dirt can be vacuumed up. Foot sweat would have to be shampooed out."

"May I come in?" asked Friday, glancing over the librarian's shoulder to where her picture was pinned to the notice board.

"Of course you can," said Mrs. Cannon. "You are an essential contributor to this assignment."

"I suppose you can just this once," said the librarian begrudgingly. "But you must all leave your bags outside."

"We don't have any bags," said Melanie. "Mrs. Cannon thinks they encourage bad posture and crushed clothes."

"That's right, Melanie," said Mrs. Cannon. "You'll be getting an A+ for your assignment now, such excellent verbal comprehension skills."

"You must also pass through the metal detector," said the librarian. "No scissors, knives, razors, scalpels, or cutting implements of any kind are allowed in the library. Is that understood?"

The class just stared at her blankly.

"I think she would like you to respond verbally," said Mrs. Cannon. "I'll count you in. On three, give her a hearty 'Yes, ma'am.' One, two, three . . ."

"Yes, ma'am," chorused the class.

The librarian glowered at them all. "Very well. Chen, you watch the door. You people, come this way." The librarian walked to the end of the circulation desk and led the class through the metal detector, across the library, past the stacks and the individual study desks, and to the back wall, where there was a small room housing the school archives.

When they arrived at this door, the librarian took a large key ring from her pocket and started searching through the keys. Eventually she found the pink key with a picture of a fluffy duck on it and opened the door, flicking on the lights.

Friday had never been in the archive room before. There were filing cabinets along one wall, two tall rows of bookcases housing an impressive collection of leather-bound books, and along the far wall a row of glass display cases. Everything looked perfectly neat and ordered, as though no one had ever come in here, which Friday suspected was the case. School was boring enough in the present—archival records of the school from decades earlier took boringness to a new level.

"Over here," said the librarian, leading the way to the glass display cases. "There!" she said, pointing to a large leather-bound book. "The official Highcrest Academy book of records."

The class gathered around and peered in through the glass. The open page contained a list of punishments given out for student infractions. There had been no suspensions back in those days. Justice had come in a precisely counted number of strokes from the paddle.

The librarian opened the glass lid, took out the book, and handed it to Mrs. Cannon, who laid it on the nearby reading table and flipped through to the last page.

"Please, you should be wearing gloves," said the librarian.

"Here we go," said Mrs. Cannon, arriving at the back page. "Hang on, where is it?" She flipped back and forth, then checked the cover. "The map is missing!"

"It can't be," said the librarian, taking the book herself and flicking through to the last page (even though she wasn't wearing gloves). "But that's impossible. This room is always locked, and so is the case. There is only one key for each lock, and those keys are always in my pocket."

"May I see the page?" asked Friday. "Or, rather, where the page was." She reached out to take the book.

"Gloves," snapped the librarian, nodding toward a box containing white cotton gloves.

Friday pulled on a pair, privately reflecting that the only crime she had observed so far was that the librarian had not been locked in a mental asylum. The librarian handed her the book, and Friday carried it over to the reading desk in the middle of the room, where she peered closely at the inside of the spine.

"Someone cut it out," Friday announced.

"Impossible," said the librarian. "No cutting implement is allowed inside the library. Scissors, knives, box cutters—they are all strictly prohibited. When I first came here all these wealthy entitled students were cutting pictures out of the encyclopedias to stick in their school projects. They didn't even realize what they were doing was wrong because it was what they always did at home. That's why I had the metal detector installed."

"Really?" asked Melanie. "I always thought it was because you were afraid someone would become enraged by a library fine and make an assassination attempt."

"Someone must have torn it out," said Ian.

"No," said Friday. "There are no dog-eared tear marks. This is an old book. The paper was made in an old-fashioned way. You couldn't tear a page out perfectly." She reached into her pocket and pulled out a jeweler's eyepiece (made of plastic so it had gone past the metal detector). Friday bent down and looked very closely at the page.

"Don't breathe on the paper fibers," pleaded the librarian.

"If you want her to solve the case, she will have to breathe," said Mrs. Cannon.

"Then try to make them dry breaths," said the librarian.

"This is very odd," said Friday. Her face was only millimeters from the page she was looking at. "I can see the very thinnest remnants of the page from where it was removed. But it's strange. It appears to be cut because the line is so straight. But it also appears to be torn because, on a microscopic level at least, the fibers are ragged where the page was removed."

"And look at that," said Melanie.

"What?" said Friday.

"The last punishment entry on the last page," said Melanie, pointing to the book. "E. M. Dowell and A. J. Dean—"

"That's the Vice Principal," interrupted Friday.

"They each got six strokes of the paddle," continued Melanie.

"For what?" asked Ian.

"It doesn't say," said Melanie. "It's torn off."

"The rest must be on the back of the stolen map," said Friday.

"Or perhaps the map is on the back of the stolen evidence of the Vice Principal's wicked past," suggested Ian.

"Intriguing," said Friday. "Anyway, it proves that the Vice Principal was lying when he said he didn't know E. M. Dowell. They got up to some sort of mischief together."

"Who cares?" said the librarian. "That was years ago. I want to know who vandalized my book now!"

"Let's see what we can uncover," said Friday. "Everyone out of the way. I need to search the room, and I don't want any more disturbance to the dust particles or carpet fibers until my investigation is complete."

Friday got down on her hands and knees and began systematically crawling up and down in neat lines, as if she were cutting a lawn with her knees. The whole time she kept the jeweler's glass in her eye, and occasionally she would bend down until her nose brushed the carpet for a really close look.

This process took a while, which annoyed the librarian. She had just glanced at her watch for the ninth time and was about to snap "Is this really necessary?" or "Why are you wasting my time?" when Friday suddenly yelled "Aha!," dropped down flat on her face, and stretched her fingers underneath a filing cabinet.

"What is it?" asked the librarian.

"We'll see," said Friday. She was stretching as far as she could but couldn't quite reach. "Do you have a pen?" she asked.

"Students aren't allowed to have pens in the library," chided the librarian. "Not since the time Ian Wainscott wrote a defamatory retort in Winston Churchill's *History of Britain*."

"Churchill was overweight," protested Ian. "It's a historical fact."

"I just need something long and skinny," said Friday.

"I'll tip it back for you," said Melanie, stepping behind the cabinet, grabbing it by the top, and tilting the whole four-drawer structure backward.

"Don't do that—it's heavy!" exclaimed the librarian.

"I've got it," said Friday as she reached under the cabinet.

"Oops," said Melanie as the weight of the filing cabinet became too much for her. She stepped aside and the whole thing crashed on the floor.

"What have you done?" wailed the librarian.

"Sorry," said Melanie. "I'm in a low percentile for upper-body strength."

"Never mind that," said Friday. "Look what I've found."

Everyone turned to see what Friday was holding in her hand.

"Big whoop, it's a piece of string," said Mirabella.

"Yes," said Friday, rubbing the string between her fingertips, "but more importantly, it's a *damp* piece of string."

"What has that got to do with anything?" demanded the librarian. "So the janitor has been negligent in cleaning under the filing cabinets. Even I, one of the few sticklers for proper standards and rules left in this school, cannot get upset with a janitor for missing a small piece of string hidden unreachably far underneath a filing cabinet." The librarian turned on Melanie. "Dropping a filing cabinet full of artifacts unique to the school history is, however, a different matter."

"But this piece of string is how the thief stole the map," said Friday.

"What are you talking about?" asked the librarian.

"First we need to ask: What do we know about string?" said Friday.

Mirabella and her friends groaned.

"Here we go," said Ian.

"Someone be a dear and fetch me a chair," said Mrs. Cannon. "I'm guessing this is going to be a lengthy explanation, and my legs don't like standing for prolonged periods."

"This type of one hundred percent cotton string is commonly used in cooking," said Friday. "Being cotton, it is highly absorbent."

The librarian rubbed her temple as she struggled to contain her rage. "It's times like this that I wish the Headmaster would approve my request to have security guards assigned to the library," said the librarian. "Preferably armed ones."

"What else is string?" asked Friday.

"It's handy if you can't find your shoelace," said Peregrine.

"Yes, but mathematically," said Friday, "the beautiful thing about a piece of string is that if you make it taut"—Friday held both ends of the string and pulled them tight—"it forms a perfectly straight line."

"What has that got to do with the stolen map?" demanded the librarian.

"The map was cut out of the book," said Friday. "It's impossible to get a cutting device into the library. But water is the enemy of paper."

"It is?" asked Melanie.

"Yes," said Friday. "Paper is just pressed wood pulp. It's more of a physical bond than a chemical one. If you add water to paper, the paper absorbs it and expands, weakening the physical bonds that hold the paper whole. That's what the thief did. He or she took this piece of string, stuck it in their mouth, walked into the library perfectly innocently, picked the door lock and then the cabinet lock, took the piece of string out, pulled it taut, laid it along the paper, and let chemistry do its work."

Friday demonstrated, placing the damp string across a page and holding it down. "The paper was weakened in a perfectly straight line so that it almost fell out of the book." She pulled the next page out, neatly separating it from the spine.

"A perfect cut," said Melanie.

"You did it again!" exclaimed the librarian.

"Well, I had to demonstrate," said Friday.

"You vandalized the book!" shrieked the librarian.

"But I haven't stolen the page," said Friday. "You can Scotch-tape it back in."

"Scotch tape?! Scotch tape?!" The librarian's face was turning so red it looked as if she could have some sort of cerebral failure at any moment.

"Perhaps we'd better leave," said Melanie.

"Good idea," said Mrs. Cannon. "After all our work on this assignment, we'd better go back to the classroom and reflect on what we have learned."

"Does that mean we can nap, ma'am?" asked Peregrine.

"Of course, my dear boy," said Mrs. Cannon. "But do try to dream about literature so that the Vice Principal can't accuse you of wasting your time."

"That was odd," said Melanie as she and Friday lagged behind the others on their way across the quad, back to their classroom.

"I know," said Friday, taking out a lollipop so that she could mull over the problem. "Who would have thought that a librarian could have such terrible anger management problems? I think they should allow yelling in the library. The librarian obviously needs to blow off more steam."

"No, I mean it was odd about the map and the string," said Melanie. "It seems like an awful lot of effort to go to for not very much. If you were going to break in somewhere, why not break into the school office and steal some money? Or better yet, break into the kitchen and steal the leftover peach cobbler?"

"I'm going to send this off to be DNA-tested," said Friday, holding up the string.

"But how will that help?" asked Melanie. "We don't have DNA on every student in the school."

"No," agreed Friday. "Curse those ridiculous privacy laws. But I'm working on that."

Chapter

17

Kidnapped?

Friday and Melanie were, again, sitting in a very boring school assembly. Melanie had been sound asleep for half an hour. She always nodded off as soon as everyone sat down after singing the national anthem.

Friday was trying to use her impressive and immense powers of concentration to tune out the Vice Principal's speech on the wickedness of chewing gum, but she was struggling because he spoke with a strange and dramatic intonation that misled you into believing he was about to say something much more interesting than he actually was. Friday gave up and started counting the planks of wood in the ceiling.

She had just gotten up to 158 and was gaining a newfound respect for the problems facing quantity surveyors, when the back doors of the hall burst open and a freshman boy rushed in.

"Chen has been kidnapped!" exclaimed the boy.

Friday was electrified by the announcement. Finally, something interesting was happening. But she was shocked by the response of the teaching staff and student body. They collectively groaned and went back to listening to the Vice Principal's speech.

"Sit down, boy," said the Headmaster. "We'll deal with Mr. Chen's amateur dramatics later."

Friday was agog. She had to sit there for another half hour wondering what on earth was going on. Kidnapping was usually considered one of the most grievous categories of crimes. In countries that had the death penalty, it was the type of crime you could get the death penalty for. Friday elbowed Melanie in the ribs. She had to talk to someone about it, even if they could only whisper.

"Wake up," whispered Friday.

"Is assembly over?" asked Melanie.

"No, but Chen has been kidnapped," said Friday. "Remember him? He's the library monitor. I wonder if the librarian did it herself. She seems to overreact wildly to the most minor infractions. Perhaps he got a food smear on a book and she flew into a rage."

"Is that all that happened? I'm going back to sleep, then," said Melanie, closing her eyes and instantly dropping off.

Friday elbowed her in the ribs again. "Why is no one concerned?"

"About what?" asked Melanie.

"About Chen being kidnapped?" said Friday.

"Oh, because it happens all the time," said Melanie.

"The poor boy is repeatedly kidnapped?" asked Friday.

"No, he stages his own kidnapping," said Melanie with a yawn. "He does it four or five times a year. More often if there's a traveling circus nearby or something good on at the movies."

"But don't they see? A boy who pretends to kidnap himself would be the perfect victim for a real kidnapping," said Friday.

"Barnes!" yelled the Headmaster from up on the

stage. "I can see you talking. Stop it. See me after the assembly."

Friday went bright red with embarrassment as every student in the school turned to look at her. Ian caught her eye and wagged his finger at her like she'd been a naughty little girl. Friday turned to Melanie, but she'd already dropped off to sleep again.

Friday could see why Melanie never got in trouble. As far as teachers were concerned, she was the ideal student. She never interrupted or asked difficult questions, and they never had to grade her assignments because she never handed them in.

Friday waited by the back doors for the Headmaster to come out and yell at her. But when he emerged, he was not alone. Rodda, the boy who had interrupted the assembly, was keeping pace with him and frantically talking.

"But it's different this time," said Rodda.

"That's what his note says every time," said the Headmaster.

"But he didn't leave a note," said Rodda.

"Of course not, there's no need," said the Headmaster. "I can just photocopy the last one."

"But you've got to do something," said Rodda.

"I shall," said the Headmaster. "I will call Mrs. Flynn at the sweetshop and tell her to send him home immediately when he goes in for his peanut butter cups."

"But that's what I'm trying to tell you," said Rodda. "Chen already has a ten-pound jar of caramel balls in our room. His aunt Stephanie sent it to him yesterday. He has no reason to stage his own kidnapping and go into town."

"I'll call the movie theater, then," said the Headmaster.

"The only film showing is a documentary," said Rodda.

"Really?" said the Headmaster. "That doesn't sound like Chen's cup of tea."

"It's got subtitles," added Rodda.

"He definitely won't be there, then," said the Headmaster. "I saw his grade for his English report. Comprehension is not a strength of his."

"Would you like me to investigate?" asked Friday.

The Headmaster spun around. "Barnes, I might have known you'd be eavesdropping."

"You asked me to wait for you," said Friday.

"Yes, there's always a clever excuse, isn't there?" said the Headmaster grumpily.

"If Chen really has been kidnapped this time," said Friday, "it would be very bad for the school's image, especially if your response in the first critical hour was to sit through the rest of assembly, then go back to your office and eat chocolate cookies."

"How dare you . . ." blustered the Headmaster, before curiosity got the better of him. "How did you know I was going back to my office to eat chocolate cookies?"

"You are under a lot of pressure from the Parents' Association, whose members are concerned about the holes on the school grounds and the subsequent

upswing in ankle injuries," said Friday. "They are applying pressure through the Vice Principal. And you've just had to listen to him give a thirty-minute speech. It must gall you that he has the audacity to talk at great length when he isn't even headmaster, which must make you wonder if he will soon be headmaster, which must be upsetting. And, given your waistline, you are evidently a man who seeks comfort from emotional problems through eating. You are a principal, so it wouldn't do for a man of your executive stature to eat a normal plain cookie. Therefore I deduced a chocolate cookie was more likely. You probably have a large supply in your desk drawer, from parents bribing you to turn a blind eye to their child's appalling behavior."

The Headmaster rolled his eyes. "Why can't somebody kidnap *you*?"

"I'd love it if they did," admitted Friday. "I've always wondered what it would be like. Trying to escape would be much more of a challenge than most of the things they get us to do in PE."

"I haven't got time to deal with this now," said the Headmaster, looking at his watch. "I have a phone conference with the school council. We've only got a half-hour window of opportunity when the time zones work, so I can't delay. The president of the council is in New

York, the treasurer is in Tokyo, and the secretary has hiked out of the Amazon rain forest to use a pay phone." He hurried away.

"What about Chen?" Friday called after him.

"He'll turn up," said the Headmaster. "He always does. Unfortunately."

The Headmaster disappeared into the administration building. Rodda sobbed.

"Are you crying?" asked Friday.

"No," sniffed Rodda.

"You're about to," said Friday.

"I don't want Chen to be kidnapped," said Rodda.

"Because you're such good friends and you'll miss him?" guessed Friday sympathetically.

"Yes, but mainly because I'd hate to have a new roommate," said Rodda. "I don't suppose I could pay you to come and investigate?"

"How much?" asked Friday.

"As many caramel balls as you can find," said Rodda.

"Deal!" said Friday. Lollipops were her preferred sweet, but she was prepared to be open-minded.

"Did someone say 'caramel balls'?" asked Melanie, who had just caught up with Friday. "Can I come, too?"

And so they hurried off in the direction of the boys' dormitory.

Chapter 18

The Open Window

"What are you expecting to find in their room?" asked Melanie as they hurried to the boys' dorm.

"Well, Chen is a boy," said Friday, "so I'm guessing the room will be messy, smell funny, and have obsessive iconography tacked to the walls."

"What?" asked Rodda. "Why do you say that?"

"All pubescent boys have two things in common," said Friday. "Number one—their feet smell bad. Number two—their developing neural pathways cause them to think obsessively about something that is totally unimportant. For example, some boys obsess about football; others obsess about music. But Chen is not like that. He is a library monitor. I'm guessing the object of Chen's irrational obsessive devotion is in the field of science fiction or perhaps even fantasy role-playing games."

They stopped at the dorm room.

"How did you know?" asked Rodda.

Friday and Melanie stepped inside. There were Star Wars posters on the walls, Lego models of fictional spacecraft, and an extensive library of books relating to the playing of Dungeons and Dragons—all exactly as Friday had predicted.

"Have you been in here before?" asked Rodda.

"Thankfully, no," said Friday as she sniffed the air and noted that she was right about the smell as well.

Chen's desk was littered with textbooks and notebooks, all covered with repetitive mathematical scrawl. In the center of it all, in pride of place, stood an enormous half-eaten jar of caramel balls.

"Which is Chen's bed?" asked Friday, although as she looked at the beds, she immediately knew. One bedspread was beige. The other featured a life-size picture of a Time Lord.

Friday walked over and checked under the bedding. It seemed silly, but experience had taught her that eliminating the silly was an important part of any investigation. If she started sending off samples for DNA testing while Chen, who was merely a slim boy, was taking a deep nap under a thick feather comforter, then she would feel very foolish indeed. But Chen was not to be found in the bed, under the bed, or in the wardrobe.

"How does he escape when he usually feigns a kidnapping?" asked Friday.

" 'Escape' isn't really the right word," said Rodda. "There's no barbed wire or electric fences. He just leaves."

"So how does Chen usually 'leave'?" asked Friday.

"It depends," said Rodda. "Sometimes he jumps into a bush and runs off when we're out on the field during PE. But if we're here in the dorm, he just climbs out the window."

"But the window is closed," said Melanie.

Friday went over to look. The window showed a beautiful view. There was a gravel driveway that trucks used as an access road to make deliveries to the dining room. Beyond that was a pristine green lawn surrounding a huge maple tree that was bright red with autumn color, and through the half-naked branches Friday could see the hockey field and the baseball diamond beyond. She shoved the window open.

"Hang on, you might need this," said Rodda, holding out a ruler to Friday.

"Why?" asked Friday, taking it.

"The sash is a bit tricky," said Rodda. "Sometimes it falls shut when you least expect it. If the ruler isn't there, any vibration can make it drop suddenly."

"Interesting," said Friday, wedging the ruler between the sill and the sash. She stuck her head out the window and looked right, then left, closely inspecting the gravel driveway.

There wasn't much to see except for some tire tracks, which could have been made at any time. Friday was just drawing her head back inside when she noticed something on the window frame above her. She awkwardly twisted herself around, almost into a limbo position, so that she could look up at it.

"Oh no!" exclaimed Friday, clapping one hand over her eyes as she used her other hand to steady her blind reentry to the room.

"You've found something?" asked Rodda.

"Yes, I have—proof that Chen was indeed taken away," said Friday. "You'd better fetch the Headmaster."

"What is it?" asked Rodda.

"See for yourself," said Friday. She stepped away from the window and did not turn to have another look herself.

Rodda peered at the reddish brown stain on the sash, which had strands of something sticking to it. "What is it?" he asked.

"I take it Chen had black hair?" asked Friday.

"Yes," said Rodda.

"Then that is a bloodstain with a little bit of hair stuck in it," said Friday.

Rodda's eyes bulged, then rolled up into his head as he fainted.

"Wow," said Friday. "He's even more squeamish about blood than me."

"I'll go and get the Headmaster," volunteered Melanie.

"Thank you," said Friday. "And try to bring him along without the Vice Principal. This could get embarrassing."

An impressive three minutes later, which showed that both Melanie and the Headmaster must have been walking quickly, a thing neither of them liked to do, the Headmaster burst into the room. The trouser leg above his left knee was torn and dirty.

"What is the meaning of this?" he demanded, expecting to confront Friday in full-detective mode, crawling along on the floor with a magnifying glass. Instead, he discovered her kneeling on the floor and holding Rodda in her arms. "What's going on?"

"Ah, Headmaster," said Friday, "you've fallen into another hole, I see."

"That's beside the point," said the Headmaster. "Explain yourself."

"Rodda fainted," said Friday, standing up and letting Rodda drop to the floor. "I found blood and hair on the window sash, consistent with the injury you would get if you banged your head very hard on the timber."

"So you're saying," said the Headmaster, "that Chen actually *has* been kidnapped?"

"Headmaster," said Friday, "there is no need to alarm yourself. Chen does apparently have a serious head injury and he has been taken away. But he has not been kidnapped."

"Now is not the time to talk in riddles," said the Headmaster.

"You will find Chen unconscious and lying on the green waste pile at the local dump," said Friday.

"What are you talking about?" demanded the Headmaster.

"Let me explain what happened," said Friday.

"Please do," snapped the Headmaster.

"Chen is a silly but academically able boy," said Friday. "From his desk we can see that he was studying for a math exam next week. His family is supportive of his academic goals. His aunt even sends him his favorite sweets to help him focus. Studies show that a high-sugar diet aids short-term memory. If you want to improve the school's academic standing, you should think about handing out candy bars for exams."

"Don't wander off the point," chided the Headmaster.

"Sorry, where was I?" said Friday. "Ah yes, Chen was at his desk studying dutifully when he went over to the window, opened it, and stuck his head out. Why would he do that?"

"Perhaps he wanted fresh air," said the Headmaster.

"Chen likes playing Dungeons and Dragons," said Friday. "He clearly has no interest in fresh air."

"I don't know, then," said the Headmaster.

"Let us ask ourselves 'What is a window?'" said Friday.

"Please, just get on with it," said the Headmaster, rolling his eyes.

"A closed window is an entrance for light into a room," continued Friday. "But when you open a window it becomes a porthole for communication."

"For goodness' sake, just tell us what happened!" demanded the Headmaster.

"Chen opened the window to yell at someone outside," said Friday.

"How can you know that?" asked the Headmaster.

Friday stood back. "Look out the window yourself. What do you see?"

"The driveway, the tree, the lawn," said the Headmaster.

"Exactly," said Friday. "There's something missing."

"Chen," said Melanie.

"Something missing in addition to Chen," said Friday. "Where are the autumn leaves? That maple tree has shed half of its leaves. Thousands of them would have been dropping off every day for the last few weeks. Where are they?"

"Mr. Pilcher, the caretaker, was working on this side of the school this morning," said the Headmaster. "He would have collected them all. It's his job to keep things tidy."

"And how do men like to keep autumn leaves tidy in this day and age?" said Friday. "Not with the quiet dignity of a rake, no, they use leaf blowers. A device powered by a gas engine with no muffler to deaden the sound. So poor Chen sat here trying hard to study, while the groundskeeper was out there going on and on with his leaf blower in the Sisyphean task of collecting up autumn leaves in a school with over a thousand deciduous trees."

"What are you saying?" asked the Headmaster.

"I'm saying that Chen, delirious from studying and empowered by the large amount of sugar pumping through his bloodstream, stuck his head out the window and yelled at the caretaker," said Friday.

"Mr. Pilcher didn't report anything," said the Headmaster.

"Of course not," said Friday. "He was using a leaf blower—he couldn't hear anything. In fact, he would have been wearing ear protection; occupational health and safety would require it. Frustrated, Chen withdrew his head, just as the slippery window dropped down. The speed of his retreating head combined with the speed of the frame moving down would have been quite a blow. Force equals mass times acceleration. His head bounced away from the window frame, he toppled forward, and landed down there."

"On the driveway?" asked the Headmaster.

"No," said Friday. "Because there was something else there. The caretaker's truck, full of autumn leaves from his morning's work. Since the truck was full, he would have taken it straight to the dump, which is where you will find Chen."

"Oh my goodness!" cried the Headmaster, taking out his mobile phone and dialing. "I hope you're wrong. Being dumped unconscious at the dump is almost worse than being kidnapped. At least if he was kidnapped, it would be someone else's fault."

"I'm sure he's fine," said Friday.

"As long as they haven't put the load through the mulcher yet," added Melanie.

"I hadn't thought of that," admitted Friday.

"I've got to get down there," cried the Headmaster, and for the first time in twenty years he ran—out of the room and to his car, as quickly as possible.

Chen returned to the school two hours later with a bandage wrapped around his head and a second, even larger, jar of caramel balls. When asked, he claimed he could not remember what had happened. But from the autumn leaves tucked down the back of his collar, Friday knew she had been entirely right.

The Art of Disorienteering

Friday and Melanie were waiting with their classmates by the edge of the swamp. A sophomore class, including Christopher, was milling around as well. Mr. Maclean, their geography teacher, was about to stage his annual fall semester assignment. He was forcing the students to take part in orienteering. There was a general air of glumness about the group. Geography was bad enough already without adding physical exercise into it.

"Ah, good morning, geographers," called Mr. Maclean as he strode across the field, a warm cup of coffee in one hand and a bag full of athletic equipment in the other. "Are you ready to put theory into practice in the great outdoors?"

"No," said Mirabella sullenly.

"Can I be excused, sir?" asked Peregrine. "I'm allergic."

"To what?" asked Mr. Maclean.

"Nature," said Peregrine.

"Me too," said Melanie.

Other students started putting up their hands.

"We all are," claimed Judith.

"This is sooo not relevant to our lives," said Mirabella. "The only type of map I want to be able to read is the floor plan at the mall. Why can't we do orienteering there?"

There were murmurs of agreement among the group.

Mr. Maclean ignored them. "You will each be given a map of the school grounds and an orienteering card," he explained. "Your job is to use your map to find five markers. At each marker is a unique punch. You use the punch to put a hole in your card. When you have all five punches you return here."

"And this constitutes how much of our final grade?" asked Friday.

"One hundred percent," said Mr. Maclean. He was very proud to have thought up a way of grading two whole classes of his students all at once, and without having to read any term papers. (He'd been taking tips from Mrs. Cannon.) "I've prepared a list of teams. Step forward to see who you're partnered with; then collect your equipment and you can start. The first pair back here with their card fully punched automatically gets an A++."

Before Friday had time to react, Ian leaped forward. He glanced at the list. "Melly Pelly, you're with me."

"Goodness, no," said Melanie. "Couldn't I swap and get someone slower-moving?"

Ian ignored the question, snatched up the equipment, grabbed Melanie by the hand, and took off into the forest at a sprint.

"Poor Melanie," said Friday. "I don't think she's going to enjoy this."

"Come on, let's go," said Christopher as he turned to Friday.

"Go where?" asked Friday.

"Orienteering," said Christopher with a smile. "We're a team."

"We are?" Friday noticed Christopher was already holding a map, compass, and card. "Of course, sorry, my mind stepped out for a moment."

"Should we follow Ian?" asked Christopher.

Friday took the map and looked at it. "We could if we wanted to fall off a cliff in about three minutes' time. If we want to get to the first marker alive, better to take a slightly longer route and go this way." Friday led Christopher into the swamp.

"Are you as good at reading maps as you are at everything else?" asked Christopher as they walked swiftly through the bush. Friday was not going to run anywhere, not even for an A++.

"Yes," said Friday.

"Let me guess," said Christopher. "From years spent in the Girl Scouts?"

"Goodness, no," said Friday. "I would never be involved in an organization whose sole motivating philosophy is based on acquiring cloth patches. No, I learned how to read maps on summer vacation with my family."

"Really?" asked Christopher.

"My mother read an article on the educational benefits of an outdoor experience," explained Friday. "So she arranged for our whole family, including my four older brothers and sisters, to go on a two-week kayaking trip."

"You could cover a lot of ground in two weeks," said Christopher.

"My mother is a conscientious woman," said Friday. "She made sure to find a very long river."

"So what happened?" asked Christopher.

"A helicopter dropped us upriver," explained Friday. "We were supposed to spend the entire trip paddling down to the estuary. But there was a flash flood on our second night and all our kayaks were swept away."

"And you took charge of the situation?" asked Christopher.

"You have to understand," said Friday, "that my parents and my brothers and sisters all have PhDs in theoretical physics, so they have absolutely no practical life skills at all. If they had to guide a rocket to Pluto using the gravitational pull of Jupiter as a slingshot, my family would have no problem doing the mathematics. But moving in a straight line through non-theoretical obstacles is beyond them. I walked out, found a town, and called the helicopter back to pick up the rest of the family."

"Dramatic," said Christopher.

"We never went on a family vacation ever again," said Friday. She didn't know why telling this story brought a lump to her throat. The last thing she wanted to do was cry in front of Christopher.

Christopher nudged Friday so that she would look up at him. "You know, sometimes you seem older than I know you are," he said softly.

"So do you," said Friday, looking into Christopher's eyes.

"Ah, that's because of my terrible past." He grinned.

"You were wicked?" asked Friday, smiling at Christopher's attempt to lighten the mood.

"I had to repeat freshman year because of 'behavioral issues,'" said Christopher unrepentantly.

"What behavioral issues?" asked Friday.

"I'll tell you later. Look, there's the first marker," he called, having spotted the orange-and-white flag up ahead. They hurried toward it.

"It looks like we're going to be first," said Friday.

"No, you're not," said Ian as he brushed past at a

sprint, beating them to the flag, finding the control punch, and punching a hole in his card.

"Hey, where's Melanie?" asked Friday. "You didn't lead her over the cliff, did you?"

"No, I asked her if she wanted to sit under a tree taking a nap while I ran around getting all the punches," said Ian. "Unsurprisingly, she agreed." He raced off again. But as he did, he brushed past Christopher, causing him to drop his compass. Then Ian, far from accidentally, ground the compass underfoot.

"Hey, you broke our compass," Christopher yelled. But Ian had already disappeared into the bushes. "I'm going to get him."

"Don't worry," said Friday. "I've got a wristwatch. We can use that and the sun as a compass."

"How?" asked Christopher.

Friday took off her watch and laid it on her palm. "If we line up the twelve with the sun, then north is halfway between the twelve and the hour hand. That way!"

Using Friday's careful assessments of the best route to take across the landscape and her accurate map reading, she and Christopher had all five holes punched in their card in under one hour and ten minutes.

There was a slight delay at the fifth marker because Friday could not get the punch to work properly. It didn't help that she had sweaty palms as a result of unaccustomed exercise combined with unaccustomed proximity to a very handsome boy.

Fortunately, Christopher had big strong hands (one of the characteristics of his attractiveness) and was able to take a firm hold of the punch, cutting through the card with a minimal amount of squeezing and wrestling on the handgrip.

"Come on, let's run back to the finish," said Christopher. "Perhaps we'll win."

"I'm sorry," said Friday. "I'm not very good at running."

Christopher smiled. "You can do it. I'll help you." He took Friday by the hand.

Friday was surprised. No boy had ever held her hand before. It didn't tingle like in the romance novels, but it did feel nice in an inexplicable, visceral way. Christopher's hand was large and rough compared with hers. He tugged her hand and took off running. Friday found she quite enjoyed being dragged through the forest.

The terrain wasn't difficult. There was a fire track

to follow, which they ran along for five minutes. Friday had never run for so long in her life. She seriously began to worry that she might suffer from some sort of cardiovascular failure.

"Stop," cried Friday, yanking her hand free and coming to a complete halt.

"We can't stop now," said Christopher. "We're so close. Look over the treetops—you can see the top of the flagpole on the main building."

It was a struggle for Friday to speak while she was breathing, or, rather, attempting to breathe, so hard.

"No," panted Friday. "I mean"—more panting—"it'll be quicker if we go directly through the bush."

"Also more dangerous," said Christopher.

"I like to live dangerously," said Friday, finally gaining some control over her respiration.

Christopher smiled and grabbed her hand again. "Let's go!"

They started thrashing their way through the undergrowth. Six minutes later, they stumbled out the other side of the forest onto the edge of the football field. They were both covered in mud, scratches, and insect bites. And Friday's brown cardigan had so many pulled threads it was even uglier than usual.

"We made it," said Friday.

They looked around. Mr. Maclean was standing on his own.

"We're going to win," said Christopher. "Come on!"

Friday and Christopher started running again. But they had taken only a few steps when Ian and Melanie burst out of the bushes ahead of them. They both had leaves and dried grass all over their backs. Ian was actually carrying Melanie, and he was running full tilt. Friday and Christopher ran as fast as they could, but even with the large weight to carry, Ian had such a big lead he easily reached the finish line first.

"Well done, Mr. Wainscott. Miss Pelly, interesting

approach," said Mr. Maclean. "But I suppose all's fair in love and geography. The A++ goes to the two of you."

"Thank you, sir," said Ian with a smile. "I'm just sorry that in the noble pursuit of academic excellence there has to be winners and losers. And yet there does."

Friday rolled her eyes.

"He cheated," accused Christopher.

"That's a shocking allegation," said Ian. "Sir, surely you should dock his grade for making defamatory statements."

Mr. Maclean confronted Christopher. "Can you prove that?"

"No," said Christopher. "But I know that he did."

"If you can't back it up, don't make the accusation," chided Mr. Maclean. "Or you'll end up with a B."

"I can prove it," said Friday.

Chapter 20
Proof

If you've got proof that Wainscott cheated, then spit it out," said Mr. Maclean. "Otherwise, I'm giving you both a C for unsportsmanlike behavior."

"Just look at him," said Friday. "The course is five miles over difficult terrain. He isn't puffed or sweaty. Even with moderate exercise, the human body will start to sweat after just ten minutes."

"What can I say?" smirked Ian. "I'm in superb physical condition."

"He doesn't have scratch marks on his legs or insect bites," continued Friday. "But he does have dirt, leaves, and dried grass on his back. In fact, so does Melanie."

"I do?" said Melanie.

"Neither of you look like you've been running through the bush for the last hour," said Friday. "Instead, you both look like you've been lying on your back among leaf litter and dirt."

"I have," agreed Melanie. "Friday is very clever with her deductions, isn't she?"

"Yes, she is," said Christopher.

"That's nonsense," said Mr. Maclean. "Wainscott has every square punched on his card, using the different unique control punches."

"May I see his card?" said Friday.

Ian smirked again. "Be my guest."

Friday studied it intently. His card certainly did have all five squares punched.

"I think you'll find everything in order," said Ian.

"Chris," said Friday, "let me see our card."

"Oh, it's 'Chris' now, is it?" said Ian, raising his eyebrows. "I saw you two holding hands as you burst out of the bushes. Perhaps we should be asking what you two were doing in the bush for over an hour."

Friday ignored Ian and looked at her own card. "I

suspected as much," she said. "Mr. Maclean, did you organize the same end-of-term assignment for your class last year?"

"Yes, of course," said Mr. Maclean. "I always send my class out orienteering in the autumn term."

"So Ian knew that this test was coming up," said Friday. "He's had plenty of time to contact an orienteering organization and order his own set of control punches, then hide them in the bushes so that he could leave Melanie, make a show of arriving at the first marker, and then sneak back to his hiding spot, punching the other four holes, before going back to Melanie and finishing the challenge."

"That's very far-fetched," said Mr. Maclean.

"And entirely unprovable," said Ian.

"Look at his card," said Friday. "Every single punch mark is cleanly cut."

"Proving I went to every marker," said Ian.

"No," said Friday. "Proving that you *didn't*. Because the punch on the fifth marker was blunt—it chewed the card. We had to punch it several times to get it to work. You did not punch this hole with the same punch we did."

"I can't be punished because I was able to make a tricky punch work better than you did," said Ian.

"No, perhaps not," said Friday. "Because Mr. Maclean is a lazy man who would prefer not to take this further."

"Excuse me?" said Mr. Maclean.

"I don't mean it as an insult, sir," said Friday, "just an observation of fact. But definitive proof would be if I found where Ian hid his box of control punches."

Ian just laughed.

"It would be like trying to find a needle in a haystack," said Christopher.

"Harder," said Ian, "because in this case the needle is not there."

"Perhaps," said Friday. "But it must be hidden somewhere fairly obvious. Near a landmark that is easily identifiable from a distance, or any angle." She scanned the treetops. One tree stood higher than the others. It was the Great Oak, the first tree planted by Sebastian Dowell when he founded the school.

"There," said Friday. "The Great Oak."

"You mean, we've got to go hiking again?" asked Melanie.

"You didn't go hiking the first time," said Friday.

"No, but if I had," said Melanie, "I'd be most put out."

"I am not going traipsing through the forest, looking for hypothetical false punches," said Mr. Maclean.

"Why not?" asked Friday. "It would be good exercise for you."

"I have to wait here for all the other students to return," said Mr. Maclean.

Just then Peregrine and Mirabella burst out through the bushes. They were both bedraggled. They looked like they'd spent a month camping in the wilderness, not an hour going for a walk.

"The others aren't coming back," announced Mirabella.

"What?" asked Mr. Maclean.

"They've all given up," said Peregrine. "They're refusing to move until you send in a helicopter."

"There you go," said Friday. "The best use of your time now would be to call the emergency services on your cell. Get them to send a helicopter to start looking for the missing students. While we're waiting, we can nip over to the Great Oak and look for the punches."

Even with the apathy of Mr. Maclean and Melanie to contend with, it only took the group five minutes to hike over to the Great Oak.

"This is quite the wild-goose chase, Barnes," said Ian. "I'm thinking of lodging an official complaint for harassment."

"You set me up on terrorism charges," said Friday. "You can hardly get on your high horse when I simply call you out for cheating. Which I know you did, by the way. That's the difference. You've been naughty— I haven't."

"Just because you don't actually make ricin in your dorm room doesn't mean you aren't extremely irritating in many other ways," said Ian.

"I don't know how you have the energy to argue," said Melanie. "All this walking is exhausting."

"So where are these punches, then?" asked Mr. Maclean.

Friday scanned the clearing around the Great Oak. "We have to think like Ian," she said.

"I doubt you have the imagination to conceive what goes on in my brain," said Ian.

"I don't need to know all the goings-on," said Friday. "Just the bits about where you would hide a set of punches."

"In the ground," suggested Christopher.

"No," said Friday. "Digging would be too much like hard work."

"Under a bush," suggested Melanie.

"No," said Friday. "Too easy to stumble across. The

best hiding spot would be somewhere only Ian could find it. And what unique skill does Ian have?"

"Handsomeness," suggested Melanie.

"In addition to handsomeness," said Friday. "He is a superb acrobat."

"Really?" asked Christopher.

"Oh yes," said Melanie. "His father was a graduate of the Barnum and Bailey Circus Skills University. That was a key fact Friday used to prove he committed a bank robbery and have him thrown in prison for seven years."

"Your dad is in prison?" said Christopher. "Which prison?"

"I'd prefer not to discuss my personal issues with anyone at any time," said Ian, "but particularly not with you now."

"He thinks of such clever, rude things to say," said Melanie. "Friday, you're so lucky to have found him."

"Given his acrobatic skills," continued Friday, "the best place for Ian to hide the punches would be somewhere high up in the tree."

"And how are you going to prove that?" asked Ian. "We all know you're barely capable of jogging, so you aren't going to be able to climb the tree yourself. You can't cut down the tree either, because it's protected. So what does that leave? You'll have to train a squirrel to search for you."

"I'll be your squirrel," volunteered Christopher.

"This is getting better than a Danielle Steel plot," said Melanie.

Ian made a scoffing noise.

"Are you sure?" asked Friday. "The lowest branch is eight feet off the ground. And you are pretty . . ."

"Short," Ian said, finishing off her sentence.

"I may not be an acrobat, but I do know a thing or two about climbing," said Christopher. He walked over to the trunk and stared at the bark for a few moments.

"Are you trying to out-think the tree?" Ian asked.

Christopher ignored him. He kicked off his shoes, reached up, wedged his fingertips into the small gaps in the bark, pulled his feet up off the ground, and tucked his toes into the bark. After a few swift, decisive movements, he had pulled himself up to the lowest branch.

"Wow!" said Melanie. "He must have really strong fingertips."

"And toe tips," agreed Friday.

"Climbing is a hobby of mine," called Christopher. "It's all just a matter of working within the laws of physics."

"I think he's using science talk to flirt with you," said Melanie.

Once Christopher was in the branches, climbing became much easier, and he soon disappeared from sight.

Friday glanced across at Ian. He was starting to look sullen.

"I've found a bag," called out Christopher. "It's tied to a branch."

"What's inside?" asked Friday.

"A box," called Christopher.

"And what's in the box?" asked Friday.

There was a rustle of leaves and suddenly Christopher dropped to the ground, landing with the agility of a cat, right in front of them.

"See for yourself," he said, handing Friday the box.

She opened it. Inside was a brand-new shiny set of orienteering punches.

"You can't prove they're mine," said Ian. "I was framed. She planted them up there."

"What I don't understand," said Friday, "is why on

earth you would want to cheat. If you'd just done the orienteering properly, you probably would still have won."

"Most people at this school don't care about grades," added Melanie.

."I have to," said Ian.

"What does that mean?" asked Friday.

"I need all the A's I can get," said Ian. "I have to maintain my grade point average or I lose my scholarship."

"But you're the second-smartest student in the year, after Friday," said Melanie. "Surely your grade point average is fine."

"Second smartest isn't good enough, is it?" said Ian. "When there's only one scholarship."

"I don't need the scholarship," said Friday. "I've already got ten thousand dollars toward next term's fees."

"Oh, and you think you'll keep stumbling across crimes to solve and be rewarded for, do you?" asked Ian. "One per semester for the next five and a half years?"

"I don't see why not," said Friday. "It's worked so far."

Mr. Maclean sighed and rubbed his eyes while he tried to figure out what to do. "Barnes, you and

Gianos will get the A++ for finishing first," he finally said.

"Yes!" exclaimed Christopher.

"Wainscott and Pelly," said Mr. Maclean, turning to Ian and Melanie, "I'm giving you a B+."

"What?!" exclaimed Christopher. "Aren't you going to send Ian to the Headmaster? He cheated!"

"He did have sufficient geographic knowledge and initiative to seek and purchase a set of orienteering punches. Most students wouldn't even be aware that such a thing existed," said Mr. Maclean. "And he managed to go into the forest, find the oak tree, and make his way back without getting lost, which may very well turn out to be the second-best result in the class. And I can't give everyone F's."

"That's ridiculous," protested Christopher.

"Actually, I think it shows remarkable good sense," said Friday. "Very uncharacteristic for Mr. Maclean. Well done, sir."

"I'd say thank you, Barnes," said Mr. Maclean, "but I don't think that was really a compliment."

DNA Results

It took Friday's legs several days to recover from the ordeals of orienteering.

"Ow," said Friday as she gingerly got out of bed. "Exercise is bad enough when you're doing it, but it hurts afterward as well. Indeed, from my observation, it hurts more on the third day than it does on the first."

"I know," agreed Melanie. "It's a wonder fit people manage to walk at all."

"I imagine if you exercise regularly your muscles get used to it," said Friday.

"How awful," said Melanie. "I never want to find out."

As they headed out to breakfast, Friday and Melanie came across a large group of giggling girls gathered in the lobby of their dormitory.

"What's going on?" asked Friday.

"The police are on their way!" said Mirabella. "They're going to be here all afternoon."

The girls giggled again.

"What for?" asked Friday.

"They're looking for that escaped convict," said Trea. "They've been searching the whole region. Today they're searching here."

"They're bringing all the recruits from the police academy to comb the grounds," said Mirabella. "Just think, hundreds of fit young men everywhere, searching for clues. I'm going to skip English so I can go and watch."

"You'd better be careful, Friday," said Trea. "They might arrest you again."

The giggling erupted into cackling.

"Enjoy your objectification of men in uniform," said Friday. "We're going to breakfast."

"There's a letter for you," said Melanie, noticing an envelope in Friday's pigeonhole near the doorway.

"Really?" said Friday, taking the official-looking envelope and inspecting the letterhead as she headed out the door.

"Who's it from?" asked Melanie.

"It's from the university medical lab," said Friday. "It's my test results."

"I didn't know there was something wrong with you," said Melanie, "apart from the obvious social malfunction, and I doubt that could be measured in a blood test.

"No, it's the results from the DNA test on the string," said Friday. "The piece we found in the library. I got one of my mother's former PhD students to run it through for me."

"Your mother is a theoretical physicist," said Melanie. "Why would she have a student working in a DNA testing lab?"

"The student changed her major," explained Friday. "After one semester of working with my mother, she grew to hate all things relating to quantum mechanics generally and M-theory in particular."

As they walked across to the dining hall, Friday tore open the envelope and began reading the cover letter. "I don't believe it," she said. "They found an exact match."

"I thought you couldn't match DNA unless you had a sample from a suspect," said Melanie.

"You can't," said Friday. "If they found a match, that means the saliva must belong to someone associated with the university who voluntarily allowed their sample to be available."

Friday flipped through the rest of the paperwork, looking for the name.

"Let's see," said Friday. "It's a female, Anglo-Saxon Celtic, no genetic diseases, called . . ." She found the piece of paper with the name. "Friday Astrella Barnes."

"What a coincidence," said Melanie. "The thief is someone with the same name as you, apart from the middle name. You'd never have such a ridiculous middle name."

"My siblings are called Quantum, Quasar, Orion, and Halley," said Friday. "Of course I have a ridiculous middle name!"

"Does it start with an 'A'?" asked Melanie.

"Yes," said Friday.

"It isn't Astrella, is it?" asked Melanie.

"It is," said Friday.

"That's either a really big coincidence," said Melanie, "or they found your spit on that string."

"I think the probability of my spit being on a piece of string at a crime scene is much greater than two sets of parents each thinking it was a good idea to name their daughter Friday Astrella Barnes," said Friday.

"But how did your spit get on that string?" asked Melanie.

"I don't know," said Friday.

"Do you remember licking any string?" asked Melanie. "Do you think it is possible that you could have cleverly and elaborately broken into the library, stolen the map, and then entirely forgotten about it?"

"No," said Friday.

"You could have been hypnotized," suggested Melanie.

"That's not possible," said Friday. "When I was eight I hypnotized myself and implanted instructions in my subconscious to never allow myself to be hypnotized again."

"So what did happen?" asked Melanie.

"Someone must have stolen my spit," said Friday.

"But who would do something so unhygienic?" asked Melanie. "And weird?"

"Ian," said Friday. "He's trying to get rid of me to protect his scholarship."

22

The Confrontation

Ian!" called Friday angrily as she strode across the dining hall with Melanie following.

Ian looked up from the paperback he was reading as he ate his bacon and eggs. "Not you. Can't you see I'm busy?"

"Doing what?" asked Friday. "Plotting to have me arrested again?"

"Reading *The Curse of the Pirate King*," said Ian. "It's very good. Lots of violence."

"Did you steal my spit?" demanded Friday.

"Has she lost her marbles?" Ian asked Melanie.

"She doesn't play marbles," said Melanie. "At least, I've never noticed that she does."

"You put my spit on that string," accused Friday.

"I wish I had," said Ian, "if I had known it would make you this angry."

"Friday!" Christopher called out from the other side of the hall.

Friday and Melanie turned.

"It's your other boyfriend," said Melanie. "It really must be exhausting for you to be in a love triangle."

"I'm not in a love triangle, or even a love straight line," protested Friday.

"Then why is the second-cutest boy in the entire school running over here to talk to you?" asked Melanie.

"Chris isn't the second-cutest boy in the school," said Friday.

"You think he's the cutest?" said Melanie. "Oh dear, Ian will be disappointed about that."

"I've had as much of this conversation as I can handle without taking anti-nausea medication," said Ian as he tucked his book into his pocket. "I'm going." He slouched away.

"Fine," Friday called after him. "But this isn't over. I'll prove it was you."

"Friday," said Christopher as he caught up with the girls. "I need your help."

"How romantic," said Melanie.

"Melanie, perhaps you'd better go on to class," said Friday. "I'll help Chris and catch up with you as soon as I can."

"You want privacy," said Melanie. "I understand. I would say I would take notes for you in math, but of course I won't, and I'd hate to lie." She drifted away.

"What's the problem?" asked Friday.

"You'll have to see for yourself," said Christopher. "It will be easier than trying to explain."

Christopher took Friday by the hand, which Melanie would have noted made her blush, and hurriedly led her outside.

"Where are we going?" asked Friday.

"You'll see," said Christopher. He squeezed her hand tighter. If Friday had wanted to let go, she would have found it hard to do now.

They turned around the corner of the building, and there on the gravel stood Mr. Pilcher's riding lawn mower.

"A riding lawn mower?" said Friday. "You know fixing machines isn't really my thing. Don't get me wrong—I have an excellent grasp of the workings of the internal combustion engine. But I am clumsy, and if I stuck my hands under a lawn mower, chances are I would cut my fingers off."

"I'm not going to cut your fingers off," said Christopher.

"I didn't think you were," said Friday.

"I'm going to break your arm if you don't shut up and get on that riding lawn mower right now," said Christopher.

Friday turned and looked him in the eye. Christopher smiled his most charming smile.

"Did you just say you would break my arm?" asked Friday.

"Yes, I did," said Christopher. "And I'm not going to repeat myself. If you don't do as you're told, I'm just going to do it."

Friday evidently had a look of disbelief on her face. While Christopher did not repeat himself, he apparently saw a need to explain. "You're not the only one who knows about physics. I, for example, know that Archimedes stated that with a fulcrum and a lever he could move the world, which is how I know that if I used my knee as a fulcrum and your forearm as a lever I could snap your elbow like a dry twig. Now, would you like to get on the lawn mower?"

Again, Christopher smiled. It crossed Friday's mind that perhaps he didn't know what he was saying. That perhaps English was his second language and he had learned the wrong sentence from a phrasebook, but as she looked at him she could see that while his face was smiling, his eyes were cold and dead inside.

"All right," said Friday. She climbed onto the lawn mower.

"Not onto the seat, you idiot," said Christopher. "I'm not letting you drive. You can sit on the grass catcher."

Friday

climbed over the seat onto the grass catcher. Christopher got in and turned on the engine.

"Let's go. We don't have much time. The police will be here in an hour," he said. "But first, I don't want you trying anything brave during the ride." Christopher produced a zip tie from his pocket and fastened Friday's hands to the grass catcher. He put the lawn mower in gear and took off across the football field.

"Someone from the school is bound to see us," said Friday. "A noisy diesel engine is hardly a subtle escape vehicle."

"If someone sees us, they won't think anything of it," said Christopher. "You do strange things for the Headmaster all the time. And I am very charming. Everybody loves me. They will assume I'm helping you out as a Good Samaritan.

Or that I'm mowing the lawn for Mr. Pilcher. Either way, they won't interfere."

Friday looked back at the school. The buildings seemed to grow smaller as the lawn mower steadily chugged away. Through the windows she could see tardy students hurrying to their classes. Not one of them looked her way.

They crossed the football field and went down an embankment, nearly tipping the mower over. Christopher was not a cautious driver. He drove onto the soccer field and powered toward the tree line of the swamp in the distance. The mower could go at an impressive speed when the blades were up. They must have been traveling at fifteen miles per hour, which was fast enough for Friday to not consider trying to get free and jump off.

The lawn mower wound around trees with reckless speed. It scraped a pine tree at one point, causing the grass catcher to shudder so hard that Friday was worried it would fall off.

"Mr. Pilcher is not going to be happy about you scraping his lawn mower," said Friday, noting the ugly marks on the paintwork.

Christopher just laughed. "I couldn't care less." He

smashed through a rhododendron bush and headed straight for a mangrove tree.

"Stop!" cried Friday.

Christopher yanked on the hand brake and jumped out in one fluid movement. Friday toppled forward and landed on her back in the driver's seat with her hands still tied to the grass catcher.

"Ow," said Friday.

"Your clumsiness knows no bounds," said Christopher with a sigh. "Come on, sit up. I need you to read something for me."

Friday struggled to get herself up in a sitting position. The best she could manage was to sit sideways in the driver's seat.

"What can I read that you can't?" asked Friday. "Is it something in Latin? Or Lithuanian? Or perhaps scrambled by the Enigma code?"

"It's a map," said Christopher. He went over to a hollow log, reached in, and pulled out a wad of paper. He unfolded it and held it in front of Friday.

"The stolen map of the school!" exclaimed Friday.

"Well done, Sherlock," said Christopher sarcastically.

"Why are you showing it to me?" asked Friday.

"And why is it such a mess?" As Friday looked at the map she could see it had suffered hard use. It had dirt stains, frayed edges, and even a mysterious red blotch. "Is that a bloodstain?" she asked.

Christopher looked over the top of the map to see what she meant. "No, that's strawberry syrup from when Mrs. Marigold served sundaes for dessert." Christopher pointed to a brown stain in the corner. "That's a bloodstain."

"Good to know," said Friday.

"I need to find the 1987 time capsule," said Christopher.

"Why?" asked Friday.

"That's none of your business," said Christopher. "You're the one tied to a lawn mower. I ask the questions. Now look at the map and tell me where it is."

Friday studied the sheet of paper being held in her face. The diagram of the school grounds was fairly detailed for a hand-drawn effort. Scattered across the page were numbers indicating where the different years had buried their time capsules. Most of them had been crossed out.

"You've been digging up the time capsules," stated Friday. "And you crossed them out as you went along.

That's why holes have been appearing all over the school."

"Congratulations, you figured it out," said Christopher scathingly. "I can see why you have a reputation for genius."

"The Headmaster fell in the 1999 hole. Jacinta fell in 1991. Ian in 1980," said Friday, fascinated to see such an accurate map of all the minor incidents of the last few weeks.

"Look, the map says 1987 should be here," said Christopher, stabbing the page with his forefinger. "But I've dug and dug, and I can't find it. You tell me where it is."

Friday looked at the spot where Christopher was pointing. It was where they were standing, along the edge of the swamp. Friday looked around. She now noticed there were muddy holes in the ground. Holes everywhere. She looked at the map again.

"No wonder you have such rough hands," said Friday. "You must have been out here digging every night of the week."

"Look, right by the '1987' there's a

skull and crossbones and two beans drawn under-neath," said Christopher.

"That's a pirate symbol," said Friday.

"So?" said Christopher.

"Pirate maps are written in code," said Friday.

"I knew it," said Christopher.

"It's a very simple code," said Friday. "You're going to kick yourself for not working it out."

"Just tell me," said Christopher.

"On a pirate map you reverse everything. At least that's what they always do in *The Curse of the Pirate King*," explained Friday. "Left means right, right means left, up means down, and down means up."

"Okay," said Christopher. "So how does that help us?"

"If you're looking for the '87 time capsule," said Friday, "dig up the '78. The reverse."

"I did dig up the '78 capsule!" exclaimed Christopher. "I've dug up all the seventies and all the eighties."

"How deep did you dig?" asked Friday.

"Deep enough to find the capsule," said Christopher.

"Then you didn't do what the map said," said Friday. "Those aren't baked beans. They're footprints. One above the other. It means two feet. So you reverse the year and dig two feet. The '87 capsule was buried *below* the '78 one."

"You're kidding me," said Christopher. "That's just silly." He was clearly getting very angry.

"But that's just it, isn't it?" said Friday. "This was done by kids. Twelve- or thirteen-year-olds. Kids think like kids."

Christopher snatched the map out of Friday's hands and looked at it again. "The 1978 is in the middle of the Headmaster's rose garden!"

"I bet they enjoyed that," said Friday. "Doing it right under his nose. Although it would have been the former Headmaster. The current one started in 1989."

"Someone is going to notice if I start digging up the rose garden again in broad daylight," said Christopher.

"So wait for nightfall," said Friday.

"I can't," said Christopher. "There are going to be two hundred police cadets swarming over the grounds in an hour."

"Quite the predicament," said Friday.

"I need a diversion," said Christopher.

"It'll need to be an impressive diversion," said Friday. "Something that will have the whole school looking the other way long enough for you to dig a two-foot-deep hole in the rose garden and find the capsule."

"So what would you suggest, Einstein?" asked Christopher.

Friday sighed. "Einstein was a theoretical physicist, therefore just the person to speak to if you wanted to invent a nuclear bomb. But he would have been wildly unqualified to make suggestions about petty crime. The man didn't even brush his hair most days. Practicalities were beyond him."

"Just shut it with the trivia facts and tell me what you suggest," said Christopher.

"Why should I help you?" asked Friday.

"Because you don't want me to drive this lawn mower into the swamp with you tied to it," threatened Christopher.

"Okay, good point," said Friday. "I'd pull the fire alarm. The whole school will be evacuated to the football field for roll call. The rose garden is on the far side of the school. That will give you at least ten minutes, perhaps fifteen, to dig up the 1987 time capsule."

A few minutes later Friday and Christopher were crouched in the bushes at the far side of the hockey field from the rose garden, scoping out the scene.

"The nearest switch for the fire alarm is in the entrance," said Friday. "Miss Priddock, the school secretary, is incredibly dim-witted and unobservant, but I think even she would notice if someone pulled the fire alarm directly opposite her desk. You'd be better off looping around to the far side of the school and grabbing the fire pull at the rear of the boys' dormitory. Boys never notice anything."

"Give me your hat," said Christopher as he snatched the green porkpie hat from Friday's head.

"Hey," cried Friday. "That's my trademark accessory."

"It's about to be my diversion," said Christopher. He opened the gas cap on the lawn mower, screwed Friday's hat up, and jammed it inside.

"That is going to be terrible for the felt," cried Friday. "I'll never get the smell out."

Christopher pulled out the now-gasoline-soaked hat. "Stay here," he instructed.

"That's a bit redundant given I'm still tied to this grass catcher," said Friday.

Christopher scanned the area in each direction, then stepped out of the bushes and calmly walked over to the administration building. As he crossed the shrubbery, Friday saw him bend down and pick up a large rock. He went over to the window of the school supply store and threw the stone through the lowest pane. The window shattered. Then Christopher produced a lighter from his pocket and set Friday's hat alight.

"Nooooo!" cried Friday.

Christopher threw the flaming hat through the

broken window, then calmly walked back to the bushes where Friday was tied up.

"How could you?" demanded Friday.

"I'm sure the school is insured," said Christopher.

"Not the school, my hat!" wailed Friday.

"Come on, I'm doing you a favor," said Christopher. "That was one ugly hat." He turned and looked back at the building. Smoke was starting to waft out the broken window. "It won't be long now."

Sure enough, two seconds later the fire alarm started wailing.

They could hear people yelling, followed by the general shuffling associated with three hundred people starting to move at once.

Christopher climbed back onto the driver's seat of the lawn mower. He waited until the noise of people moving had just about died down, then he turned the engine on and sped toward the rose garden, mowing down a whole bed of Lady of Shalott Rose-blooms before coming to a stop. He opened up the lawn mower's storage compartment and took out a spade. Then he took something out of his pocket. Friday wasn't sure what it was until he released the safety catch.

"Pruning shears?" said Friday. "What are you going to do? Trim the roses?"

"Shut up," said Christopher as he lunged toward her.

Friday closed her eyes. If she was going to be stabbed, she would rather not watch. But Christopher simply cut the zip tie holding her hands.

"You're letting me go?" asked Friday.

"Yes, because I'm secretly a really lovely person," said Christopher, again with his sarcastic voice. "No, I'm making you dig the hole, idiot."

"You want me to dig a hole two feet deep in under ten minutes?" asked Friday. "Then you're the idiot."

"Just do it," ordered Christopher. "I need to keep a lookout. It's freshly turned earth. It won't be hard, even for you."

Friday raised the spade and speared it into the ground. It was a well-maintained tool.

"This is Mr. Pilcher's, isn't it?" said Friday. "You're the one who staged the bunya-bunya pine attack, just so you could get this spade."

"I thought it was an inspired idea," said Christopher. "The best thing about using a tree as a patsy is that it can't rat you out."

"No, Mr. Pilcher's hat did," said Friday.

"I didn't realize the track team were such early birds," said Christopher.

"Why did you put my DNA on the string?" asked Friday as she kept digging. "That was just weird."

"It's your own fault for being such a meddler. I had to try to get you out of the way," said Christopher. "The plan was to find the string myself and put the police onto you. You would've been expelled for sure."

"But how did you get my spit?" asked Friday.

"You remember when the science club did a study on oral bacteria?" said Christopher. "And we all had to spit in petri dishes?"

"You stole my petri dish?!" exclaimed Friday.

"It's always useful to have a DNA sample handy," said Christopher. "If you think you might need to frame someone, that is."

Friday's spade hit something hard. Christopher heard the noise. "That's it," he said. "Get it out."

Friday tapped around until she found the edge of the container. Then she slid in the spade a little deeper and levered it out. Christopher took the spade from her while she bent down and pulled up a large white cardboard box. The box had the words "Apple Pie" written neatly in the center.

"Oh dear," said Friday. "I think I know what this is."

"Let me see," said Christopher, snatching the box away from Friday. "It can't be a pie."

"No, it's something much worse," said Friday.

Christopher opened the box. There was a horrendous smell. "A dead cat?!" He gagged.

"It's Purrcy," explained Friday.

"That's disgusting," said Christopher. "Is this the time capsule?"

"No, this is just some lazy home economics students' attempt to hide evidence," said Friday. "The time capsule will be deeper down, two feet under." She kept digging until her spade hit something else. Something more solid. She levered out a dirty copper box with the number "87" etched clearly on the top.

"At last," said Christopher.

"What now?" asked Friday.

"Open it," said Christopher.

Friday crouched down with her back to Christopher and started to jiggle the rust-encrusted latches. "The lock is rusty," said Friday. "It would be quicker to use a—"

"Watch out!" cried Ian.

Friday spun around to see Christopher swinging the flat of the spade toward her head. She ducked and closed her eyes, then heard a thud. It took a second for her to realize it was not a thud against her skull. It was the thud of Christopher hitting the ground. Ian had knocked him over and they were wrestling among the rosebushes.

"Ow!" cried Christopher. "I've got thorns in my back."

"You'll have my fist in your front in a minute," said Ian.

"Don't!" cried Friday. "He's got a weapon."

"Thank you," said Christopher. "I forgot about that." He whipped out the pruning shears.

"Didn't your mother ever tell you not to play with gardening tools?" asked Ian.

"I think there are a lot of moral lessons Christopher failed to learn from a parental figure," said Friday.

Ian backed away from him.

"What do you know?" said Christopher. "The two smartest kids in school. But you're not smart enough to outwit a pair of pruning shears, are you?"

"Well, clippers are an inanimate object," said Friday. "They have no intelligence, unless you are anthropomorphizing them, in which case I don't follow the gist of your analogy."

"Shut up," said Ian and Christopher in unison. They started circling each other.

"Don't be a hero, Ian," Friday warned.

"Don't you mean, don't be *any more* of a hero?"

asked Ian. "I did just crash-tackle a guy who was about to hit you in the head with a spade."

"I just don't want you to get hurt," said Friday. "If shears can cut through a rose stem, I hate to think what they could do to a blood vessel."

"You've got a really high opinion of yourself, don't you?" accused Ian. "That you think there is even a possibility that I might risk injury for you."

"Well, I am standing in a rose garden watching two boys fight over me," said Friday. "My self-esteem is on the upswing."

All this time Christopher was edging away. He climbed back up on the lawn mower. "You stuck-up rich kids make me sick," he said.

"Actually, we're the two poorest kids in school," said Friday. "Ian is the scholarship student, and I pay my way because my parents earn barely enough to afford pens and notebooks."

"Just shut up," said Christopher, "before I give up trying to make a getaway and come back to snip you." He put the lawn mower in gear and took off, lumbering back across the football field and toward the forest.

"He's getting away," said Friday.

"Good," said Ian. "The nasty upstart. I never want to see him again."

"But he's got the time capsule!" said Friday.

"I feel sorry for a boy who is prepared to commit serious assault just to steal a twenty-year-old school assignment," said Ian.

"You don't understand," said Friday. "What's in that time capsule is worth thousands."

"Of dollars?" asked Ian.

"Yes," said Friday.

Ian didn't reply. He took off sprinting after the lawn mower.

"Try not to get hurt," urged Friday. She ran after him, going as fast as she could, but Friday's run was less effective than most people's jog.

Christopher was steadily gaining speed as he approached the edge of the sports field. There was no way Ian was going to catch up with him. Friday racked her brain, trying to think of some way she could stop Christopher. If she'd had her rocket, she could've aimed that at the gas tank and blown the lawn mower out from under him. But her spare rocket was back in her room. It would take a miracle to stop Christopher now.

And then a miracle did appear, in the form of Malcolm. He burst out of the bushes at the edge of the forest and came sprinting down the slope toward the lawn mower. Christopher did not see him because Malcolm was coming in from the side. But he certainly felt him, as Malcolm launched his entire six-foot-five, two hundred fifty pounds of brawn at Christopher and knocked him off the machine. The lawn mower continued, unpiloted, into the forest. Malcolm and Christopher rolled on the ground. Malcolm pivoted himself up on top and raised his fist to deliver a blow.

"Stop!" cried Friday. "You don't want to go back to prison for manslaughter, do you?"

Malcolm clearly needed a minute to consider this. But then he decided Friday was right, because instead of hitting Christopher, he rolled him over, twisted his arm in a painful lock, and sat on him.

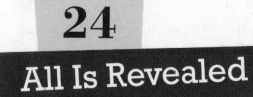

Half an hour later, Friday, Ian, Christopher, Melanie, Vice Principal Dean, and Malcolm were all sitting in the Headmaster's office. Ian and Malcolm had tied Christopher to a chair using the Headmaster's duct tape.

"What on earth is going on?" demanded the Headmaster.

"I want Ian and Malcolm arrested for assault," demanded Christopher.

"They should all be expelled for being troublemakers," declared Vice Principal Dean.

"No, Christopher needs to be arrested for theft," accused Ian.

"Actually, Christopher never left the premises with any stolen property," said Friday. "It would be hard to make the charges stick. The main reason Christopher should be arrested is because he's a prison escapee."

"What?" exclaimed everyone in the room, except for Malcolm.

"You knew?" asked Malcolm.

"I knew Christopher had been in jail since the first time I met him," said Friday. "The five symmetrical dots on his wrist are a common prison tattoo. They represent a person inside four walls."

"Really?" said Melanie. "It sounds like a symbol of someone who doesn't have the courage to get a proper tattoo."

"Why didn't you report him immediately?" demanded the Headmaster.

"I thought you knew," said Friday. "I assumed he had spent some time in a juvenile detention facility. Goodness knows, more of the privileged children at this school should be locked up. I didn't see any need to make a fuss. If he'd done his time, he deserved a second chance."

"I've had a hardened criminal enrolled in the school for two months!" said the Headmaster, shaking his head.

"The PTA is not going to be happy about this," said the Vice Principal smugly.

"Then there was the fact that Christopher was so good at climbing," said Friday. "The way he climbed that oak tree was seriously impressive. He found finger- and toeholds none of us could see. At the time, I assumed he had spent his vacations rock climbing. But when he threatened to break my arm and I realized he was in fact a violent sociopath, I recalled that the escaped prisoner had broken out of jail by climbing the prison wall."

"It's a good thing you were so observant of his impressive finger strength," said Melanie.

"The police thought Malcolm was the escapee," continued Friday, "until they discovered that the prisoner was short, brown-haired, and very young. The opposite of Malcolm. But the exact description of Christopher."

"But why would he want to enroll in school?" asked Ian. "We're only here because we have to be. Aren't prison escapees meant to run away to Brazil or somewhere exotic with beaches?"

"It's quite a coincidence, one prisoner being released on the same day another prisoner escapes," continued Friday. "Then they both come to the same place—Highcrest Academy. There had to be something drawing them here."

"Like what?" asked the Headmaster.

"The 1987 time capsule," said Friday.

"Why?" asked Ian. "Did they put gold bullion in it or something?"

"In a way, yes," said Friday. "Let's have a look."

Friday picked up the time capsule and inspected the lock.

Ian sighed. "Do we have to watch while you show off your lock-picking skills?"

"No, that wouldn't work," said Friday. "It's rusted shut." She picked up her schoolbag and rifled around inside until she drew out a ball-peen hammer. "This will do the trick."

Friday smashed the hammer hard into the lock three times. The rusty metal collapsed. She lifted the lid and pulled out a thick pile of paper. There was lined notepaper, art paper, even printed worksheets, but they were all covered in scrawling handwriting. "What is this?" asked the Headmaster. "Some kind of assignment?"

"No," said Friday. "It's a priceless handwritten manuscript."

"It is?" said the Headmaster.

"The last chapter in the final book of *The Curse of the Pirate King* by E. M. Dowell," revealed Friday.

Everyone gasped.

"The author was a student here in 1987," said Friday. "He was already working on his stories of pirates."

"Wow," said Ian, peering at the manuscript.

"Isn't that right, Malcolm?" said Friday. "Or should I call you E.M.?"

"What?" exclaimed Ian.

"Malcolm is E. M. Dowell," said Friday.

"No way," said Ian.

"How did you figure it out?" asked Malcolm.

"When the Headmaster sprained his ankle, you started for the infirmary. You knew your way around," said Friday. "And when the Vice Principal saw you he was genuinely shocked. Not because you were a scary-looking vagrant carrying his employer, but because he recognized you. You were the year above him at school. It all fit that you could be the author. You weren't in jail because you'd committed a crime. You were there to research your next book."

"What does the 'E' stand for?" asked Melanie. "Edward? Evan? Earnest?"

"Worse," said Malcolm. "Ebenezer."

"You poor man," sympathized Melanie. "I know how you feel. My middle name is Alice, and I've never been able to forgive my parents."

"So how did Christopher know about it?" asked the Headmaster.

"He was my cellmate. I felt bad for him. He's only eighteen, and he looks fourteen," said Malcolm. "Anyway, he asked all these questions about my past: my writing and my school. I thought he was just passing the time. But then his questions became more and more specific. I realized he'd read every article about me ever written. He knew all about the story of the hidden final chapter."

"This is ridiculous," said Christopher. "It's all crazy speculation. You can't believe a word of it, sir."

"I'd prefer not to," admitted the Headmaster. "But I've come to know Friday's crazy speculations are usually unerringly accurate."

"You must have thought it would only take a couple of days," said Friday. "Find the map, dig up the time capsule, sell it online to some foreign superfan, and off you go, to Brazil or Monaco or wherever well-heeled thieves congregate. But you couldn't find the manuscript; and you found yourself stuck here for weeks and weeks."

"I've got a question for Malcolm," said Melanie. "Why did you bury the final chapter? It seems like such a strange thing to do."

"I did it to irritate Archie," said Malcolm with a smile.

"Who?" asked Ian.

"Vice Principal Archibald James Dean," said Friday.

"Archie liked my stories," said Malcolm. "I found out he had handed one in as his own for English."

"Vice Principal!" exclaimed Melanie. "That is so naughty."

The Vice Principal stared at the floor, pouting.

"We got in a fistfight over it," continued Malcolm.

"Which is why you were both punished and that was noted in the records," said Friday.

"Yes, but Mrs. Cannon backed me up," said Malcolm. "She said she knew Archie hadn't written the story himself because he had less imagination than a dead geranium. Anyway, Archie was desperate to find out what happened at the end of the story, so I buried it in a secret location. Someplace I knew he'd never have the imagination to uncover."

There was a knock at the door.

"Come in," called the Headmaster.

The door opened and Sergeant Crowley walked in. "What's going on here?"

"I believe this young man may be of interest to you," said the Headmaster.

Sergeant Crowley scanned the people in the room. "Malcolm? What is it now? Not a sapphire bracelet again, I hope?"

"Not him," said Friday. "Him." She pointed at Christopher.

Sergeant Crowley peered at Christopher.

"Imagine how he would look in a bright orange prison jumpsuit," said Friday.

"Christos Stassinopoulou!" exclaimed Sergeant Crowley. "Half the region's police force has been tied up in a manhunt looking for you. They've been dredging lakes and searching abandoned mineshafts in a thirty-mile radius."

"Sergeant, before you arrest Chris," said Friday, "perhaps you could satisfy my curiosity. What crime was he jailed for?"

"We busted him for fraud," said Sergeant Crowley.

"Really?" said Melanie. "That's very unromantic. I was hoping cat burglary."

"You do realize that cat burglars don't actually steal cats?" asked Friday.

"I refuse to believe that," said Melanie.

"He used his youthful good looks," began Sergeant Crowley, "and short stature—"

"Hey!" protested Christos. "Five foot four is average height."

Ian snorted. "For a Peruvian woman, perhaps."

"He used his appearance to pass himself off as a minor," said Sergeant Crowley. "It started out with paying kids' prices at the movies and buying cheap train tickets, then escalated to him posing as the long-lost grandchild of elderly people and swindling them out of their savings."

"How was he caught?" asked Friday.

"He tried to trick an eighty-five-year-old lady awaiting hip replacement surgery," explained Sergeant Crowley. "Little did he realize she was a retired professional wrestler. She hit him over the head with her walking frame, then held him in a leg lock until the police arrived."

"She's the one who should have been doing time for excessive force," complained Christos.

Sergeant Crowley tried to pull Christos out of the office chair he was duct-taped to, but the chair just rolled across the floor. The sergeant considered the problem for a moment before turning to the Headmaster. "May I borrow the chair to wheel him away?" he asked.

"Of course, anything to help an officer of the law," said the Headmaster.

They all watched Christos get rolled out the door.

"I'll get you, Barnes!" threatened Christos. "You haven't seen the last of me."

"I'm afraid it's hard to take a threat seriously," said Friday, "when it comes from a man restrained by school supplies."

Ian closed the door on Christos before he could holler any more abuse.

The Headmaster shook his head sadly. "I can't believe he's been here the whole time. This is going to be terrible for the school's reputation."

"If it's a comfort to you," said Friday, "it's only because the school has such an excellent reputation that Christos was so safe here. Who would ever think of looking for a jailbird in the country's most expensive boarding school? And your strict enforcement of the anti-technology rules meant that none of us ever saw his mug shot on the news."

Chapter
25
Denouement

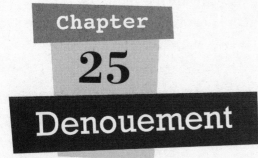

Friday, Melanie, and Ian walked back to class. They walked slowly, because they knew there was not much point getting there. They would never be able to concentrate on the lesson after the morning's dramatic events.

Ian was the first one to break the silence. "In a way," he said to Friday, "you were only able to put it all together and work out what Christos was up to, thanks to me."

"How do you figure that?" asked Friday.

"If I hadn't framed you with the ricin," said Ian, "you would never have been at the police station and met Malcolm, or heard the description of the escaped prisoner."

Friday froze and spun around to face him. "So you admit you did frame me?"

Ian shrugged. "Of course."

"Is this some sort of weird backward apology?" asked Friday.

Ian stopped walking and looked at Friday. "Maybe," he said, looking sincere for once. "I didn't want to lose my scholarship. This place might suck, with all the rules, the teachers, and kidney pie Wednesday. But home right now . . ."

"Sucks more?" Friday finished for him.

Ian nodded.

"I can relate to that," said Friday.

"Would you two like me to leave you alone?" said Melanie. "Maybe I've been watching too many day-time soap operas during vacation, but this seems to be leading to some sort of public display of affection."

"Don't be ridiculous, Melanie," said Friday.

"Who says she's being ridiculous?" asked Ian.

Friday looked at Ian. She couldn't gauge the expression on his face.

"Friday!"

The moment was broken. They all turned to see Thistlewaite, a freshman boy, running toward them.

"It's a world of high drama when you're with Friday Barnes," said Ian.

"You've got to come quickly," said Thistlewaite.

"Why?" asked Friday.

"Mr. Davies needs you in the science lab," said Thistlewaite.

"Does he need me to explain quantum mechanics to him again?" asked Friday.

"No," said Thistlewaite. "It's your father, Dr. Barnes."

"What about him?" asked Friday.

"He's turned up and taken over Mr. Davies's class," said Thistlewaite.

Friday, Melanie, and Ian ran to Mr. Davies's classroom. When they burst through the door they saw Mr. Davies slumped at a desk, holding his head in his hands while all the students looked very brain-addled and confused. Friday's father, Dr. Barnes, was scrawling equations over every last square inch of the whiteboard.

"You see, here X is a photon or Z-boson," droned Dr. Barnes, "and here X and Y are two electroweak bosons such that the charge is conserved—"

"Dad, stop!" cried Friday. "You're hurting their brains!"

Dr. Barnes looked up and adjusted his glasses. "Ah, Friday. Yes, that's why I'm here. I've come to see you."

"Then why have you taken over Mr. Davies's class?" asked Friday.

"I was looking for you and I walked past here," said Dr. Barnes, "and I saw the lesson he was teaching. He clearly needed help. His explanation was childlike."

"These are children," said Friday. "He was explaining physics to children."

Dr. Barnes turned and looked at the class. He adjusted his glasses on his nose. "Oh yes, I suppose so. I hadn't considered that."

"Why were you looking for me?" asked Friday. "You never have before. Not even the time I got lost at the shopping center and you went home without me, not realizing that I wasn't in the car."

"What?" said Dr. Barnes. "I don't recall the data you're referring to."

Friday sighed. "Of course you don't. Just tell me, why are you here?"

"Oh," said Dr. Barnes, his eyes suddenly welling with tears, his chin wobbling. "It's Dr. Barnes."

"Isn't that you?" asked Melanie.

"No, the other Dr. Barnes," said Dr. Barnes.

"Mom?" asked Friday.

"Yes, her," said Dr. Barnes.

"What's happened to Mom?" asked Friday.

"She's disappeared," said Dr. Barnes.

To be continued . . .

GO FISH

R. A. SPRATT

What did you want to be when you grew up?
An intrepid world traveler.

When did you realize you wanted to be a writer?
When a TV producer said "We'd like to offer you a job as a writer."

What's your most embarrassing childhood memory?
Why would I tell you that?

What's your favorite childhood memory?
When I was eight my mum (or *mom* as you say in America) took me to England to visit our family there. The town my English family comes from is called Dursley (it's where J. K. Rowling got the name for the Dursleys in Harry Potter), and the post office sold candy. It was all candy that was entirely different from what we had in Australia. The feeling of walking into that store for the first time must have been what Christopher Columbus felt like sighting the Americas for the first time—that a wondrous, exciting journey of discovery had just begun. They had candy in giant jars and you could pick out what you wanted. The shopkeeper would then measure it out on an old-fashioned set of scales. It was all so wonderful.

As a young person, who did you look up to most?
I'm Australian. We don't look up to people. We don't want to give them swollen heads.

What was your favorite thing about school?
I had a really nice biology teacher who let me take my shoes off in class.

What were your hobbies as a kid? What are your hobbies now?
I rang church bells. I know it's a weird hobby, but everyone in my family has been doing it for over a hundred years.

    Now I still ring church bells, but my main hobby is CrossFit. I love working out with my friends.

Did you play sports as a kid?
No. Although my mother always said that if worrying was an Olympic sport, then I could represent Australia and win the gold medal.

What was your first job, and what was your "worst" job?
My first proper job was when I left home at 18 and went to work for a pharmaceutical services company (they managed the data on drug trials) as a technical assistant (dogsbody).

    I've had a lot of truly awful jobs because I've worked in TV for twenty years. The worst ones are when the top boss forces the middle boss to hire you then the middle boss spends every waking moment trying to make you quit. Those jobs tend to involve a lot of crying.

What book is on your nightstand now?
Hah! My night stand is like a Jenga game of books. Occasionally the stack gets too high and they avalanche onto my

laundry basket. There are at least two dozen stacked on there. Plus my Kindle with another couple dozen I've got on the go. They include a lot of regency romance novels, *A Game of Thrones*, the most recent in the No. 1 Ladies' Detective Agency series, *The Candymakers* by Wendy Mass, and lots of Agatha Christie books—I just finished *Murder on the Orient Express* and started *Death on the Nile*.

How did you celebrate publishing your first book?
I got my first book contract when I was in the hospital maternity ward the day after giving birth to my first child, so I had other things on my mind.

Where do you write your books?
In my home office. I've got a very nice office. It's very messy. But I like that.

What challenges do you face in the writing process, and how do you overcome them?
The Internet is very distracting. And I am very passionate about napping. But I find if I eat enough chocolate I can stay focused long enough each day to have a book at the end of six months.

What is your favorite word?
Awesome. For two reasons: (1.) I like to be very positive. (2.) I enjoy that it irritates people. I realize that these two reasons are, in a way, contradictory.

If you could live in any fictional world, what would it be?
I really like my real world. I have an excellent life. I love Jane Austen but I would not want to live in a world with eighteenth-century plumbing.

Who is your favorite fictional character?
I don't really have just one. I really like Scarlett O'Hara from *Gone with the Wind*. Deeply unpleasant people are oft maligned in literature. And yet in real life, ruthless, driven people are the people who get things done. I always think of her when critics equate a character's flaws with a book's flaws.

What was your favorite book when you were a kid? Do you have a favorite book now?
I love the Garfield cartoons, Asterix comics, and *Hating Alison Ashley* by Robin Klein. *Persuasion* by Jane Austen is probably my all-time favorite novel.

If you could travel in time, where would you go and what would you do?
I think it takes a level of dissatisfaction with your current life that I do not have to think about these things.

I think it would be irresponsible to try and change history. And I think it would be unimaginably unpleasant to live in an earlier age when plumbing was substandard and infectious diseases were rife.

What's the best advice you have ever received about writing?
Read your work aloud during the editing process.

What advice do you wish someone had given you when you were younger?
Spelling, high school English, and storytelling are three different things. Just because you're bad at the first two doesn't mean you will be bad at the third. And the third is a tricky bit—it's like weaving a magic spell.

Do you ever get writer's block? What do you do to get back on track?
Not really. Writer's block is something you get when you can't think of anything good to write. I've spent the last twenty years swamped with deadlines. When I can't think of anything good to write I just write the best I can. But it's amazing how often, when you go back, you realize your best that day was better than you realized. You have to have faith in your own ability to practice your craft.

What do you want readers to remember about your books?
Laughing. Thinking new ideas.

What would you do if you ever stopped writing?
Become a high school science teacher.

Do you have any strange or funny habits? Did you when you were a kid?
Everything I do is perfectly normal. The things the rest of you do—that's weird.

What do you consider to be your greatest accomplishment?
Getting married. I am a very odd person. It seriously shocked a lot of people that I found someone who would want to marry me.

What would your readers be most surprised to learn about you?
In the eighties, I worked as a supermodel in Milan. (I didn't, but it would surprise my readers to learn that.)

ill Friday find her mother?

Will the students survive Dr. Barnes's lesson?

Will Ian Wainscott finally admit his
undying love for Friday?

Find out in . . .

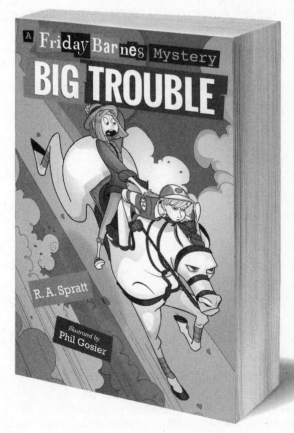

Keep reading for an excerpt.

Chapter

1

The Disappearing Doctor

Friday Barnes was running as fast as she could across the Highcrest Academy campus, which admittedly wasn't too fast because running wasn't her strong suit. She had just heard the shocking news that her father had turned up and taken over a physics lesson, and she was desperate to get to that classroom to minimize whatever public embarrassment he was undoubtedly causing.

Friday's best friend, Melanie Pelly, ran with her, and Ian Wainscott came along as well.

Ian was either Friday's arch nemesis or her love interest. Nobody was quite sure which, least of all Ian and Friday. They were inexplicably drawn to each other, but Friday had put Ian's dad in jail for insurance fraud and it is hard to get past that sort of thing in a relationship. And yet wherever there was a dramatic public confrontation involving Friday, Ian was always there.

When they burst through the classroom door they saw the science teacher, Mr. Davies, slumped at a desk, holding his head in his hands. All the students looked very brain-addled and confused. At the front of the room Friday's father, Dr. Barnes, was scrawling equations over every last square inch of the whiteboard.

"You see here, X is a photon or Z-boson, and here X and Y are two electroweak bosons such that the charge is conserved . . ." droned Dr. Barnes. He had whiteboard marker and egg stains on his saggy brown cardigan, and it didn't look like his hair had been brushed at any time in the last decade.

"Dad, stop!" cried Friday. "You're hurting their brains!"

Dr. Barnes looked up and adjusted his glasses.

"Ah, Friday. Yes, that's why I'm here. I've come to see you."

"Then why have you taken over Mr. Davies's class?" asked Friday.

"I was looking for you when I walked past here," said Dr. Barnes, "and I saw the lesson he was teaching. He clearly needed help. His explanation was childlike."

"These are children," said Friday. "He was explaining physics to children."

Dr. Barnes turned and looked at the class. He adjusted his glasses on his nose again. "Oh yes, I suppose so. I hadn't considered that."

"The family resemblance is remarkable," said Melanie.

"Yes," agreed Ian. "And it's not just the brown cardigan. It's the total ignorance of social normality."

"Not now," said Friday, before going over to her father. "Dad, why were you looking for me? You never have before. Not even the time you left me at the mall, not realizing that I wasn't in the car."

"What?" said Dr. Barnes. "I don't recall the data to which you're referring."

Friday sighed. "Of course you don't. Just tell me, why are you here?"

"Oh," said Dr. Barnes. Suddenly his eyes welled with tears and his chin wobbled. "It's Dr. Barnes."

"Isn't that you?" asked Melanie.

"No, the other Dr. Barnes," said Dr. Barnes.

"Mom?" asked Friday.

"Yes, her," said Dr. Barnes.

"What's happened to Mom?" asked Friday.

"She's disappeared," said Dr. Barnes as he dissolved into sobs.

Friday took her father outside so he could compose himself. She sat him at a picnic table with a strategically placed box of tissues in front of him just in case he burst into tears again. Melanie and Ian stood by.

"What do you mean Mom's disappeared?" asked Friday. "She can't have stopped existing. She must be somewhere."

"All I know is that yesterday morning while I was eating breakfast I looked

$$+\Delta \tau \hat{T}_o \frac{\hat{D}_x \hat{I}_o^2}{2\hbar a_o} \frac{1}{2}$$

$$N$$

$$I_{a+1,j,i}^{(t+1)} \approx \exp$$

$$N_{a+1/2,j,i}^{(t)}$$

up and noticed she wasn't at the table!" said Dr. Barnes.

"That is a bad sign," Friday said, then turned to explain to her friends. "Mom never misses breakfast. She has an alarm set on her wristwatch to remind her when to eat."

"When I reflected on the available evidence, I realized I had no memory of her sitting at the table for dinner the night before," said Dr. Barnes. "So I investigated further and discovered she was nowhere in the house."

"Wow," said Friday, "and you noticed this in under twenty-four hours? I'm impressed."

"So I called her office at the university, and she wasn't there either," said Dr. Barnes. "I'm worried that she's been kidnapped!"

"Who would want to kidnap Mom?" asked Friday.

"Theoretical physics has all sorts of practical applications," said Dr. Barnes. "She might have been kidnapped by an arms manufacturer."

"Or aliens," said Melanie. "They like kidnapping people too."

"Have you called the police?" asked Ian.

"Why? Do you think they arrested her?" asked Dr. Barnes.

"No, to file a missing person report," said Friday.

"I hadn't thought of that," said Dr. Barnes. "Is that the type of thing police do? I'd hate to trouble them if it's not their field."

"Of course it's their field," said Friday.

"I think your father is even vaguer than I am," said Melanie.

"You should call the police right now," said Friday.

"All right," said Dr. Barnes. "Do you know their phone number?"

"Don't tell me you don't know the phone number for the emergency services," said Friday.

"Why?" asked Dr. Barnes. "Is it my birth date or something?"

"It's nine one one," said Friday.

"That's not my birthday," said Dr. Barnes.

"I'll call them," said Friday. "Then we can meet the police at your house. They'll want to search for evidence before the trail goes cold."

"I don't follow. The ambient temperature is pleasantly balmy," said Dr. Barnes. "I can't see why a trail would go cold."

"It's a figure of speech, Dad," said Friday. "I'm not literally talking about a low-temperature foot-path."

"Really? Fascinating," said Dr. Barnes.

It was a two-hour drive to the Barneses' family home. Melanie went along with Friday, supposedly for emotional support, but really so she could get out of classes for the rest of the day. Friday tried questioning Dr. Barnes (her father) as he drove, but she had to give up because he was a terrible driver and it was distracting him too much. He nearly drove into an oncoming ice-cream truck while trying to remember what his wife had been wearing the last time he saw her. When they pulled up at the Barnes family's ordinary suburban home, the police were already there. They had marked off the whole front yard with crime scene tape.

"Oh my goodness!" exclaimed Dr. Barnes. "What's happened here?"

"Mother has gone missing," Friday reminded him. "We called the police about it two hours ago."

"And they've done all this already?" said Dr. Barnes. He was a university academic, so he was not used to anyone taking action with any degree of rapidity.

"Come on," said Friday. "Let's talk to the officer in charge."

They all got out of the car. Melanie and Dr. Barnes hung back while Friday ducked under the tape and started walking toward the front door.

"Stop right there!" snapped an angry-looking woman in a beige pantsuit. "If you take one more step, I'll arrest you."

Friday froze, one foot hovering midair.

"This is a crime scene," said the pantsuit woman. "With every step you take, you are contaminating the evidence."

"It may be a crime scene, but it's also my family home," said Friday, "and the missing person is my mother. If you allow me to put my foot down and continue walking into the building, I will probably be able to assist the officer in charge."

"*I* am the officer in charge," said the pantsuit woman. "My name is Detective Summers, and my experience with children is that they are anything but helpful."

"Well, you could have my father come in and have a look around to see what is missing or misplaced," said Friday. "But he is a theoretical physicist, with tenure, so he is about as aware of his physical surroundings as a dead geranium."

"That's ridiculous," said Detective Summers. "He's the victim's husband."

"Allow me to demonstrate," said Friday, turning to her father, who was still on the other side of the tape. "Dad, what day of the week is it?"

"What?" said Dr. Barnes.

"Do you know what day of the week it is?" repeated Friday.

"I suppose it's one of them," said Dr. Barnes. "I don't know . . . It will say on the calendar, I presume."

"Can you narrow it down?" asked Friday. "If you concentrate really hard, can you work out whether it is a weekday or a weekend?"

"How on earth could I be expected to know that?" asked Dr. Barnes.

"You just picked me up from school and classes were in session," said Friday. "So you should be able to deduce that it is a weekday."

"Oh yes, that line of reasoning does follow," agreed Dr. Barnes. "I hadn't really thought about it."

"What color are Mom's eyes?" continued Friday.

"Her eyes?" said Dr. Barnes. "Well, they're eye-colored, I suppose."

"Think hard, Dad," urged Friday. "You've been married for twenty-eight years. In all that time, have you ever looked at Mom and noticed what color her eyes were?"

"Blue . . . or maybe brown," said Dr. Barnes. "One of those two colors, I'd say."

"Behold my father's power of observation," said Friday.

"There must be an adult family member I can talk to," said Detective Summers.

"Yes, I do have four adult brothers and sisters," said Friday. "Quantum, Quasar, Halley, and Orion. They're all top physicists, too. You could get in touch with one of them."

"Oh no, you can't do that," said Dr. Barnes, shaking his head.

"Why not?" asked Friday.

"I tried already. I couldn't get hold of any of them this morning," said Dr. Barnes. "None of them answered the phone when I called. That's why I had to go and get Friday."

Friday was a little hurt. "I should have known I wouldn't be the first person you'd contact."

"So your four older children are missing as well?" asked Detective Summers. "And you didn't think to mention this before?"

"Could it be relevant?" asked Dr. Barnes.

Detective Summers looked like she wanted to slap Dr. Barnes. She took a deep breath, then turned to Friday. "Perhaps you had better be the one to come inside."

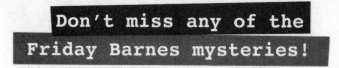